THE PROMISE THAT FADED

Elliot Parker

contents

CHAPTER 1

L ight from the young sun outside sipped through the window, the sky was bright sapphire blue and the clouds cotton white, Russle Luvré woke up, dazzled by the pale light that wrapped him in it's warm presence, he pushed his blanket aside and stretched,slowly yawning. His eyes traveled around his warmly lit room.

It is wider than necessary, a large wooden closet stood silent at a corner ,a large desk full of scracthed and crumpled paper laid opposite to his bed. His eyes finally rested on a large door made of dark wood ,he stared at it intently, expecting someone to open in anytime. And as if on cue, the door swung open revealing Lucy. The maid.

She smiled at Russle"good morning Rusty",she opened the windows and pulled the curtains open, Lucy is a stout woman past her 50's, a white apron was tied at her waist , her gray streaked hair was bunned neatly.

"good morning " Rusty said, sliding off bed.

"you better hurry,Mr.Luvré might come down in a bit" Lucy said and she strode off closing the door behind her with a gentle thud.

Rusty hurried to change his nightware into a shirt and a pair of trousers, he haistely walked out his room, the soles of his feet barely touching the cold floor, he swelled out his room into a hallway full of old oil paintings and down into a polished wooden staircase.

"where is that boy?,he is wasting my time"He heared his father's voice roar.

"there you are!" He shouted when he saw Rusty,Mr.Luvré is a tall man with a mane of long copper hair that was tamed with hair cream, his high brows had fallen, his stare sharp, his lips shrinked and thightened, he look grumpier than ever, Rusty thought.

"keep your voice down dear "Said Mrs. Luvré ,Rusty's mother, a very thin woman with stunning black hair and grimly pale skin.

"well,he shouldn't waste time"said Mr. Luvré this time lower, but features are remained sharp. A lump formed at the base of Rusty's throat.

"I'm very sorry ,father"Rusty said bowing a little to avoid his father's hot stares. He tried to swallow but the lump wont come off.

"have a seat dear,we are running late",Mrs. Luvré said gesturing to the chair opposite to her husband.

Lucy came holding a tray of pancakes with chopped strawberries and whipped cream. She gently sat down the porcelain plates, trying to make the tiniest noise possible.

"do you want anything more,Mr.Luvre sir ?"she politely asked cluthching the metal tray in her arms.

"a pot of coffee",Mr. Luvré said flatly, already started on his pancakes.

Lucy knodded and bowed, even though Mr. Luvré wasn't paying her attention, and strode off back to the kitchen.

Rusty hurried to serve himself and ate quietly, he knew the pancakes should've tasted good if not for the lump on his throat, everything tasted bland ,he was forcing chunks of foam down his mouth.

Rusty was sitting on the backseat. Up in the front was Mr.and Mrs.Luvré , the roar of the old car was the only noise heard, Rusty wanted to remain silent and if possible slowly disintegrate,he sighed and threw his gaze outside the window,their manor was now a tiny figure in the middle of a vast yellowish field,they passed on a heavily treed forest,the path they are taking was covered with fallen leaves. He stared blanky outside ,not taking care of the blurred figures that swoop passed his window.

His mind was raising ideas of leaving ,he saw himself running away from home,away from his old man's imprisoning presence,away from everything he knew.

He never felt happy with the life he have.

The car engine ceased and Rusty found himself in a middle of a vast parkway,, roaring machines are heard from the buildings not so far away , the clang of glass bottles are also noticable.

"you'll come with me today,its time you know how to operate the whole factory"Mr. Luvré said coldly, not even looking at Rusty but at his watch.

"yes father"

The factory produces milk and dairy products, milk cartoons are lined and boxed, buttermilk is bottled and corked, butter is molded and wrapped haistely by workers in a small piece of parchment.

"these machines here cork the bottles,you should keep an eye out for loose corks",he barely heard his father say over the different noises of the factory.

"come boy"his father pulled Rusty into yet another group of machines.It looks like a large barrel with a faucet for Rusty

"this,mixes the cream, the cream then turn into butter",Mr. Luvré peeked inside and so did Rusty, indeed there is butter sticking to the metal bar that mixes the cream.

"when the butter is fully and properly done,we will have ourselves it's by-product, buttermilk", Mr. Luvré took a glass bottle and opened the faucet,thick buttermilk came rushing down and filled the bottle.

Rusty knodded and followed his father as he place the bottle into a wooden case along with the other bottles.

"now,do your job"and he left without Rusty's answer.

Rusty slowly returned to the corking machines and collapsed into a wooden chair. There are other people in his station, mostly women, they stuck the luvré logo on the bottles, their movements are so synched that their bottles are done all at the same time.

Rusty returned to the corked bottles, and every now and then a loose cork catches his eye , he removes the cork and place the bottle back at the corking machine.

The light of day has weakened, Rusty was sitting again at the backseat of thier car, its leathery car seat creates noises at the smallest movement. The faint light of the redening sun outside creeps trough the car window. Occasionally a tree shadowed the light with it's thick foliage.

"Russle,the mayor's daughter will visit on Saturday afternoon for your party,be sure to be friendly,the mayor is the MOST important man "Mr. Luvré said ,making sure to emphasize how important the mayor was, his eyes ahead.

"would you like a new suit rusty ?" Mrs. Luvré asked, she stirred her head to face him, she was smiling.

"what did you call the boy Sarah?" Mr. Luvré asked her,

"It...it's rusty father" Rusty said, answering on his mother's be-half.

"who would want to be called rusty?!, I named you properly boy!,you should be thankful"

"I....I"Rusty opened his mouth to defend himself but closed it immediately, his words doesn't struck importance for his father afterall.

"rusty...I should have known and did something about it before, a Luvré cant be *rusty*"mumbled Mr.Luvré as he stirs the car.

"don't be too hard ,he's just a boy" Mrs. Luvré camly said keep-ing her voice down, but Rusty heard her perfectly.

"he is a man, he should stop acting like a boy,when I was his age ,I already can run the factory by myself,but look at him! ,vesting stupid nicknames on his self"Mr. Luvré said, he didn't even bothered to keep his voice down.

"if being a man means being like you ,then I don't wanna be a man at all" Rusty said just as loud.

"how dare you.... get out!",Mr. Luvré looked livid , he stopped the car in the middle of a dark road.

"please dear no"Mrs. Luvré begged clearly afraid for Rusty.

"no mother ,it's fine" Rusty opened the car door and hopped out smoothly. The car engine roared to life and the car zoomed away, leaving Rusty alone in the middle of the road, his only company was the silence on the forest sorounding the road.

The red light of the sun now barely touch the ground, the sky above was painted in crimson, black and blue. The clouds on the horizon glowed gold and rose.

He shoved his hands in his pockets and begun his quiet trip home, his steps were large and slow, the forest on his both sides kept quiet as he pass, the dried leaves of the forest floor rustled as his boots touch them.

The air was getting colder, he felt it enter his lungs. His breath was fast and narrow. Quickly taking in breaths. Panting a little.

After some time the forest finally ended, he reached the open field but the sky was already dark ,the waxing moon shone above and casted it's silvery light down on Rusty, stars pulsed and twinkled like a thousand small beating hearts. The tall grass of the field swayed as a gust of cold air hit him.

His black hair danced with the wind and his anger for his father soared up in the skies.

"father who?" he asked himself and rolled his eyes.He walked for another tens of minutes. Another blow of wind hit him, Rusty hugged himself as the coldness traveled down his spine.

After what he felt like hours Rusty can now see the figure of the Manor from afar. If not for the light from the windows, the manor can't be seen for it blended in so well with the dark night.

He walked rather slowly, torn between whether he would return home late or not coming home at all.

He grunted, decided he can't sleep in the wilderness. And continued his way, eyes glued on the dimly lit sky.

He reached the Manor. It was huge, it's colours are darkened by the night, its front garden was decorated with black trees and grass. The window of his parent's room is dark, only his bedroom and the kitchen remained aglow.

He hesitantly knocked on the kitchen door. After a couple of seconds the door slowly opened revealing Lucy.

"thank goodness you arrived,I was thinking of going out to find you and take you home",Lucy said in a shushed voice.

"good evening Lucy"

"good evening dear",answered Lucy smiling. "would you want me to whip something up for you?"

"yes please Im starving"

"you can wait at the dining hall",Lucy said she turned the stove on and stired the pot above it

"can I eat here?" Rusty asked, hoping that Lucy would say yes

Lucy gave him a dark look,he wasn't supposed to eat in the kitchen after all,after a moment Lucy finally answered

"you can sit here" Lucy pulled a chair and wiped the non existent crumbs off the kitchen table.

Lucy gave him a warm bowl of onion soup, Rusty muttered his thanks and started sipping it.

The soup was light and savory, it warmed his body from the inside removing all the coldness from his lungs from his unplanned night stroll.

"finish that and get to bed"Lucy patted his shoulder.

He hurrried to finish his bowl and ran upstairs , the wooden staircase was carpeted by thick velvets, Rusty was thankful . The carpet muffled his steps as he asended the stairs, he reached the corridor to his room it was pitch black .

He looked outside through a window, it must be late. The chirpings of crickets stopped. The tress were steady, untouched by wind. The moon that guided him earlier was covered in dark blankets of clouds casting dark shadows upon the blackish surface of the Manor.

Silently .Tiptoed ,Rusty walked passing the first door that leads to his parent's room. His breathing was sharp, afraid to awake his parents. Rusty glided effortly , his hands aloft. Suspended in mid air. His room was getting nearer. He crept a bit more until he was able to reach a brass knob, he slowly opened it and entered the room.

He was relieved to be here ,finally. The room was so welcoming, a warmly burning oil lamp was placed on his desk, the fire-blueish at tip danced and crumpled,the glass of the lamp had blackened. It's handle was greasy.

He blew off the lamp and blindly located his bed. He threw his body in it and inhaled deeply. His feet started to hurt. The joints on his knees felt weak and numb. His calves were pulsing, he fell asleep immediatly, tired. Both his body and mind.

"Rusty, Rusty dear ,wake up" he heard Lucy say as she shake him awake.

"I ...I "he said not really knowing what to say.

"yes you, you should get down for breakfast"

"I don't wanna see him,could you tell them I got a cold?"

"you're father won't like it, I'll bring you breakfast in a moment", Lucy said with a twitch on her thin lips.

"thanks Lucy" Rusty threw the covers back on his self again and pretended to sleep though he can't anymore.

Not long after, Lucy came with a metal tray,a bowl of porridge and a carton of milk. Lucy laid the tray on his desk and left him alone.

Rusty gleefully hopped out of bed and ate his porridge, it's warmth seemed to wrap him in a gentle embrace from the inside, undoubtedly Lucy's cooking is divine. He drained the bowl into the last spoon ,he made sure his parents were gone before he came out. Clutching the metal tray with the used bowl and glass in his hands.

The Manor is now silent. Ghost quiet . He walked down the stairs, the carpet's muffling ability had seem to weaken for he can clearly hear his own steps and the creak of the wood everytime he did so.

The Manor looked nothing like the one he seen the night before. Its walls are polished and glossy in pearly white colour. The ornamental flowers sprang to life, radiant in thier own equally stunning vases. The furnitures were velvet ,maroon. It's high celing was pristine white, brighter than the clouds outside.

He hurried to the tiled kitchen, where he found Lucy, it has a lower ceiling and peeling paint. A small door painted in blue , scratches and chippings on it's surface are evident, opens to reveal the back garden.

"I'll have a quick stroll outside" he said beaming at Lucy, and without waiting for her answer he ran towards the back door.

Cool wind kissed him as soon as he laid foot outside, he half walked half ran , still beaming at particularly no one,

He was getting farther and farther from the Manor he walked straight towards an invisible target, his mind was blanked by the hot sun, burning above him. Without knowing how far he gotten ,he reached a narrow and a not so unfamiliar dirt road.

He looked back and saw the Manor. A tiny gray dot in the middle of a yellowish field. He followed the path not caring where it would take him, the sun was burning his nape but he didn't care he wanted to be as far as possible.

"out of the way!" shouted a man riding a cart pulled by a miserable looking mule, it's short legs were bones covered in skin, it's red hair- dull and unbrushed. The animal made a grunt as it passed Rusty, leaving a trail of airborne dust behind.

"well that's one way to be nice" he frowned and continued his way, shoving his hands in his pocket. His heart beated faster, his breath grew hotter ,his throat dry. His steps slowed down, as his breathing increased. The hot sun was determined to torture him.

Under the blazing heat of the sun, Rusty walked still the dirt road. He kept his gaze down, intending not to see or know what's ahcad. Rusty heared voices, there were rhythmic clanks of hooves together with the creaks of carts. He surrendered and scanned where his feet drove him.

Rusty had reached the town, the dirt road ended and a new cobbled road took place, the street was busy ,a couple of small shops stands were settled at it's side, costumers were chatting, the indistinct chatter made Rusty felt good, it felt like freedome. Cars pass occasionally on the streets, however horse pulled caragges were dominant. The loud chaotic sound lured Rusty and without thinking he threw himself into the street his mind focused on the ice cream shop at the other side.

There was a loud crash and something hit Rusty, his gaze turned dark and blurry ,his body numb, his hearing weakened.

"somebody call help!" he heared a distant scream, . And everything darkened, he senses one by one left him.

CHAPTER 2

"T hank goodness the boy is all right"

"but who is he really?"

Rusty heard two men conversing, their voices are lowered. He opened his eyes a fraction and the image of white curtained windows formed. He opened his eyes wider and scanned his soroundings, the two men were sitting on stolls beside his bed.

"finally ,you're awake, how are you feeling?" asked the older man, smiling at him gently. His lips stretched under his thin moustache. He looks like someone n his early 20's

"I ..I'm fine,where am I?"he asked rolling his head, his eyes jumping from one bed to another

"you were hit by a car earlier"said the second man he was younger looking than the first like someone in thier late teens,he had a round and freckled face"sorry"he added guilty-ly.

"it was you?" he said, it sounded like a statement more than it did as a question.

"who are you young man?"the older man asked leaning closer.

"rusty"he started but the image of his angry father flashed in his mind.

"I'm Russle Luvré"

"a Luvré? Say, do you happen to be related to Mr.Edward Lu-vré?," asked the older man

"he's...he's my father"

"is he ?" the man was shocked.

"call Mr.Luvré this instant ,he needs to know the situation of his son" he told the younger man.

"please dont" Rusty begged lowly.

The younger man straightened and marched out of the room, gently closing the door behind him. Clearly, haven't heared Rusty.

"say Mr.Russle,hows your dairy factory?"

"it's been great"he lied, the factory experiences troubles financially, that is why his father was eager to get business partners in the first place.

"great to hear,I can't wait to sign my contract"said the man beaming at Rusty.

"wh...who are you?"

The man chuckled holding his stomach.

"of course,where are my Manners,I am Robert ,Robert Can-ior"he extended a hand for Rusty to shake, Rusty took and Shook it barely returning the mans excitement.

"he said ,he is expecting important people,and I think that's us" the younger man came in.

"and that is my brother William" Robert said, casting a backward glance at the second man.

William and Rusty exchanged curtly knods and timid smiles.

"I'm sorry Mr.Russle, but if your father is expecting us,I reckon it would be rude to keep him waiting."

"of course" Rusty said gladly.

"I called a nurse to assist you in case you need something" said William.

"thank you"Rusty bowed as the Canoir brothers opened the door and left. Leaving Rusty behind. Alone.

Silence reigned in the room, the white curtains flapped as the wind blew on it like the pristine sails of a majestic ship. He can hear the busy street outside, there was hurried footsteps and mixed tangled chatters of the townsmen, hooves of horses and screeches of un-oiled cart wheels, occasional honks of cars ,and a high pitched whistle of a passing train.

The door opened and a nurse wearing a white apron over a blue blouse swelled from it, her kind eyes contrasts to her high mocky brows.

"Mr.Luvré do you need something?"

"I...I don't ,thanks,I would like to go home" he said trying to get up. But his left hip ached, he pressed it with his palm to soothe it.

"of course,but I have to ask you not to leave alone" she smiled at him patiently.

"would you like me to call your mother?,Mr.Luvré?"

Apparently the Caniors told her, he thought. That is one of the reasons he hated his name. He felt like people treated him highly because of his name. He wanted to be treated normal, he wanted to be normal.

"please don't,can...can you call Lucy instead? She's at the Luvré Manor"

"of course ,wait here please"the nurse smiled and turned around leaving Rusty.

She came back after a moment, the smile still present on her face, she Bent down to udjust the pillow on his back.

"goodness rusty!" Lucy was screaming at the top of her lungs. She was waving her arms in the air like a swarm of wasps is attacking her. They had just arrived from the hospital. Lucy helped Rusty settle himself in a three legged stool in the kitchen.

"I...I'm sorry Lucy,it was an accident"he said.

"I know it is,but you could have died!, what has got into you?,you were supposed to be in bed suffering with your made-up sickness"

"but I am in bed,suffering for real"he said smirking

"oh child,you got me worried" Lucy said,finally able to calm down,her voice was much cooler now.

"I am..Im sorry" he stood up, resisting the pain that formed in his hip and hugged Lucy.

Lucy hugged her back. Her embrace was warm and soft like a mother's, she pated his back gently and push him back.

"off to bed dear,you need rest"

Lucy brought Rusty up to his bedroom, supporting him by the waist. The pain on his hips grew as thousand needles pricked on it in every step. She layed him on the bed and sat on the edge of it. She stared at him and stroked his black hair.

"y...you can go now Lucy,you might have something else to do"he said in a very low voice.

"none of those things are as important as you my dear,none of them " she smiled at him and caressed his bruised cheek

"but I can leave you,if you can't sleep with me watching you"

"yes please"he admitted ,smiling at her apologitically.

"very well dear, Ill bring you dinner later" she said and smoothed his hair up away from his forehead.

"th..thank you, Lucy"he said, he didn't know if he sounded grateful enough but he hoped he did, Lucy is one of the reasons he can still call the Manor his home.

Lucy struck him with one last smile and took her exit, she closed the door much gentler than she usually does. Even her footsteps sounded more muffled.

Rusty sighed lowly and burried his head on his pillow deeper. He rubbed his eyes and forced himself to sleep. He proved it hard to do, every now and then the sound of the rustling trees blewn by the wind outside his window disturbs him, he turned left and right trying to make himself comfortable.

Rusty laid in his bed for hours. Motionless. Trying to fall asleep. His hip prickled with the slightest pain. His mind wandered on his deepest thoughts and slowly, more slowly than than the sways of the tall grass blades of the yellow field , his thoughts begun to clear and blurr, he felt his body getting lighter his bed melting, his body afloat. Everything turned dull and sleep wlecomed him finally.

"Rusty... Rusty dear,wake up"Rusty heard Lucy's voice waking him, her hands patted him softly at the cheek. He opened his eyes and yawned.

He rubbed his eyes. Trying to make out his soroundings. The sky outside was magnificently painted in black and Copper, the sunset was peculiar, large strange orange clouds filled the starless sky. The yellow feild turned black so did the neigboring hills and forest. His room was lighted warmly by the blankened greasy oil lamp. He stared from the oil lamp to the lightbulb above him.

Lucy saw him staring at the bulb "Mr.Luvré doesn't want to turn on your lights,he didn't want you to have supper as well"

"I brought you dinner,come on finish it up and return to sleep immediatly" Lucy gestured to a bowl sitting at his desk.

Lucy helped her sat up and leaned his back at his bed's headboard. She handed him the bowl and Rusty hurried to finish it. He wasn't hungry at all but he feared that his father would bust into his room and find Lucy, he didn't want her to get into trouble. He scooped up the soup, almost swallowing without chewing, spoon after spoon . He drained the bowl until the very last drop.

"very good" lucy said staring at the empty bowl as Rusty handed it back to her.

She gave Rusty a glass of water, he gulped in the cold liquid ,it left a cold trace on his throat, he felt it settled on his stomach, it's coldness entering his body.

"now go to sleep,or just pretend you are" Lucy took the glass from Rusty ,blew out the lamp and quickly exited his room.

Rusty laid again on his bed, his back against the door, he closed his eyes shut trying to fall back to sleep. The sound of the night relaxed his muscles, the sublte chirps of the crikets against the strong gusts of winds that Shook the trees, the trembling leaves rattled and the twigs broke.

His door creaked open, Rusty remained silent and pretended he was asleep, he doesn't any more scolding from his father.

"oh russle"it was his mother, her voice was so low but is still noticeably cracky . She laid a soft pair of hands on Rustys shoulder. She stroked his hair with such care as though afraid that she might awaken him.

"be a good boy" she whispered on his ear. She kissed him on the cheek and something warm dropped onRusty's skin. She sniffed and Rusty knew that she was crying. She retreated and closed the door after her.

Rusty can hardly sleep that night. He awakens by the faintest sound outside. His eyelids were heavy but sleep wont come to him. He punched his pillow to a more comfortable thickness and tried again to sleep. The night grew older. Deeper. The critters outside turned silent, the ghostly song of the wind was shushed, the stars twinkled and danced on the music known only to them. The black grass outside was motionless like a vast tamed sea. The tree outside resembled a statue, hard cold and lifeless, no leaves shivered nor rustled ,no twigs Bent and bowed. Everything was frozen.

Rusty felt sleep coming to him at last. He closed his eyes and remained motionless. Then the night lulled him to sleep. Lifting his spirit allowing his body to rest.

Rusty is now sitting at the table with his parents, they are about to have breakfast. There was deafening silence ,Mr. Luvré was reading the newspaper, his face hidden behind the pages . Mrs. Luvré was staring at her lap, barely breathing, Rusty can't wait to leave the table. The silence was driving him mad.

The kitchen door opened with a bang, Rusty gave a sigh of relief, Lucy came out holding a tray of waffles. She placed it on the table and entered the kitchen once more. Disappearing from sight. Rusty forked out a waffle a bit too energetically.

Mr. Luvré snorted loudly.

Rusty's mood darkened, he chewed the waffle slowly than necessary, fixing his eyes on his plate.

Lucy appeared holding a pitcher of orange juice. Her smile warmed Rusty's inside something fluffy brushed through his stomach he returned her smile by a wider grin. Lucy hurried to pour him a glass and returned to the kitchen.

"boy!,I expect that you are ready for your party this evening?" Mr. Luvré asked his lips barely moving, his cold low voice echoed clearly on Rusty's ears.

"I ..I am"Rusty answered without looking at him.

"you must be. The mayor's daughter promised to pay you a visit,and be sure to impress her " he pointed a fork at Rusty's face before stabbing a waffle with it.

"I have your clothes prepared dear" Mrs. Luvré said, her serene eyes met Rusty's, they were smiling.

"thank you mother."he said gratefully.

Rusty was standing at their front door. The sky outside is darkening, stars are slowly appearing in the skies, the distant yellow field had turned orange, soaked in the colours of sunset. The front garden was adorned by lanterns hanged in lines above his head, turning the grass under it orangy-gold.

There were engine roars from afar, and Rusty saw headlights of vehicles trailing in the forest. He felt the air suddenly hard to breath,his heart beated abnormally, his suit tightened on his every move like a creature coiling on him sucking air out of his injured body. His necktie was choking him, no air reaches his lungs.

"she's the mayor's daughter, I must impress her.she's the mayor's daughter, I must impress her,"he repeated the thought, muttering to his self.

The roar of the car engines grew louder, the first car had already parked on the manor's pebbled walkway.

He inhaled deeply taking in the cold night's air. He plastered a fake smile on his lips and welcomed his guests, limping as he did so.

"welcome ,thanks for coming"he said, hoping he made it sound full of glee.

"thanks for the invite Russle" said Leon, the son of the school principal.

"no problem at all Leon, please do enjoy the party" he said keeping his formality, as his father wanted him.

He greeted more of his visitors, the children of pharmacy owner, the daughter of a doctor, the son of a local police officer. And Eren, the mayor's daughter, she was a beauty,her pointed face , her brown hair that shines under the lantern lights, her eyes, the colour of the fertile earth smiled at him, her pink thin lips twitched as she laid a glance at Rusty, her lilac flowery dress suited her pinkish skin.

Rusty made his way to welcome her.

"E...Eren it is a pleasure to have you here tonight" he said smiling at her

"of course" she returned his smile.

"shall we?"he offered her a hand.

She accepted it curtly and allowed Rusty to guide her to a table under a lantern, where surely everyone would see her beauty.

"the place is nice"she said as she sat down. The lanterns reflected on her own eyes.

"thanks"he muttered.

The music started playing and his father came out, he walked right into the center, beaming at everyone.

"welcome children"he opened his arms wide. "thank you for coming,remember this is your night,and I want you all to have fun so please enjoy yourselves"he knodded proudly and the music grew louder.

"I hate loud noises"Eren complained, her beautiful face was pain, her thin hands covering her ears.

"would you like to go somewhere else?"

"I would love a walk"

Rusty offered his hand to Eren, she accepted it with a smile, and they slowly made thier out the party, where the other children are enjoying theirselves, some spoiling themselves with candies and sweet beverages others dancing, touching each other's waists and cheeks.

With fast steps, Rusty limping slightly, they walked away from the Manor ,from the loud music, and away from everyone's prying eyes.

They were in the middle of the yellow field, but the night turned it black, the sky above was dark as the ground under it, it only has stars to adorn it.

A warm hand reached for his, Rusty stared at her smiling, He wrapped her hand with both of his and threw his gaze back at the stars.

"Russle ,I'm cold" Eren whispered.

Rusty stared at her, frightened, bringing her here might be not a good idea after all.

"w...we should go back then"he stood up and reached for her hands.

"no, maybe later,I want to stay here for a bit"she returned his stare, the stars on her eyes are perfectly visible.

Rusty sat down beside her, Eren crawled unto his lap ,she rested her head on his shoulder, hugging him. He felt her warm body on his chest, her slow warm breath on his neck, her hair smelled like summer flowers her skin soft and warm like fresh baked bread. He wrapped his arms around her, his heart pounded wildy.

Eren placed her lips on rusty's neck, her lips were soft and smooth and moist. He was surprised, but managed not to make any movement.

"E...Eren. Wh..what are you doing? " he asked pushing her gently away from him.

"shhhhhh"Eren shushed him, she scanned his features with her fingers, stroking his eyebrows, tracing the tip of his nose.

"the famous Russle Luvré, a lot of girls dreamed to kiss this"she said pressing his lips

"I...I don't...I don't think"

"shhhhhh,I don't want to hear anything"

She whispered, and leaned closer, their faces were now merely inches, then her lips touched his. It was soft and warm, Rusty gave in and pressed his lips deeper into hers. He wrapped her in his arms and pulled her closer, not breaking the kiss. Her hands cupped his cheeks.

Everything turned hot, Rusty's inside burned hotter than a dream but he was in a dream. He managed to pull himself together and broke the kiss, breathing deeply, catching air.

"I'm...I'm sorry Eren, I didn't mean to" he said, his voice high and frigthened

"no Rusty, it's okay" she smiled and reached for his hands

"it's okay" she reapeated.

Eren locked her fingers on his and stared at him. "the famous Russle Luvré"she cupped his cheeks and stared at him directly at the eyes.

CHAPTER 3

"The famous Russle Luvré"Eren's voice echoed on Rusty's mind,as he laid in bed, he haven't been able to sleep the night, the sun's crown is now visible at the horizon, turning the outlines of the distant mountains aglow.

Her soft lips, her demured smile, her twinkling eyes, and their kiss. It had been hours since it happened, but he can still feel her lips on his.

Rusty felt the fluffy creature on his stomach twitch and roll, he can't help but to smile, every thought that had come to him was Eren.

He lept out of bed with unnecessary glee and took a quick cold bath, the water was so cold that even his bones rattled.

Rusty hurried to dry himself, shaking uncontrollably. He patted the towel on his bare skin. Then on his hair. Until he was dry enough to dress.

He wanted to look more decent and presentable than he normally does. He put on his shirt and trousers, then laced his boots.

He scanned his self in the mirror.

A boy with dark eyes, and raven hair stared back at him, smiling with his red lips, his shoulders were framed perfectly under his white shirt.

Rusty combed his hair styling it meticulously. His lips twitche up and down as he try to master a smile.

He waited for the day to brighten, he had a quiet and quick breakfast before climbing in a different car to drive him to school. He throwed his backpack at the leather seat.

"morning Mr.Russle" the driver greeted him.

"morning George" he greeted back, George was a young man on his late teens, 18 specifically, George has been working for them for a year now, George has shoulder length blonde hair . Freckles covered his cheeks and nose.

George turned thc car's engine on, his hair swayed every time he moved. The car advanced slowly. The Peebles cracked under the car's tires, The Manor slowly grew smaller . The gardens turned into the yellowish field. As the car moves farther the field turned Wilder, the low grasses was replaced by long dry grass-blades, it's crips leaves rustled as they brush against the car's side.

Rusty can now see the forest, their path narrowed and darkened. The lush forest was preventing most of the sunbeams to reach the ground. He turned and saw the yellow field . It glowed and sparkled under the sun's bright light like a lake of molten gold.

Their car entered the forest, twigs sprout out in bushes, the branches tangled with one another, there was no way to tell which tree it belonged. The car reached the heart of the small forest,trees grew even closer,thier roots unearthed. The leaves were so thick that it seemed already dusk.

"oiiii!" George let out a high scream, a dry branch had fallen exactly at thier windshield.

"I feel like this forest doesn't like me" George said, his voice back to normal low and thick.

"looks like it" Rusty chuckled, leaning deeper on his seat.

There was light at the end of thier path. The dirt path widened little by little until the car an now glide in full freedom.

The trees thined noticeably, the branches now thinner and free, the ground was soaked in light, the leaves turned brighter, grass spruced the forest floor.

The forest ended at the top of a low hill, the car slowly declined and gained speed. Rusty's excitement grew inside him like a revolving ball of fire . The car's tires hit concrete and the ride turned smoother. Shops lined beside the street and children scattered in it's corners.

"a bit early aren't you Mr.Russle?" George asked glancing at him trough the mirror.

"oh,yeah I...I haven't slept well"he said, addressing the pair of blue eyes in the mirror.

The car slowed and Rusty picked up his bag, the school sat in front of him, it was a big school with tall iron fences and a towering gate. A bunch of children chattered at the benches near the playground, he recognised Amy Jones among them, the daughter of the bank owner.

Rusty hastily opened the door, and pulled the heavy bag up his shoulder.

"Mr.Luvré said he'll pick you up later Mr.Russle" George poked his head outside the car window, the freckles on his nose seemed to gain even more colour under the sunlight.

"yeah, th...thanks George"

George stirred the car and left, slowly disappearing from view.

"hey! Rusty !,is it true you were hit by a car?"

Rusty stirred his head and saw Duke, his best friend. Duke was a tall boy, a head taller than him, his curly brown hair burned bright under the sun

"one of the Canoirs"he shrugged, holding a hand up for a high five.

"canwa who?"Duke threw a big hand on Rusty's, making a loud clap.

"the Canoirs are one of my father's business partners,and the younger brother William hit me"

"so what's you father's say?"

"ehhhhh" he lifted his shoulders. "n...not a word they're partners afterall"

"tssssk.....tssk...tsk "Duke clicked his tounge shaking his head slowly.

"ehhhh"Rusty made a low grunt and threw his arm over Duke's shoulder. They walked through the schools playground, girls giggled and gossiped as he and Duke past.

"h...how did you know I was hit?" he forgot to asked earlier,

"Bart saw it,he was with his mother,at the ice cream shop"

There were more to Duke's story but Rusty saw Eren, Duke's wasn't that important suddenly. She was wearing a laced skirt over a flowery shirt, the style of the neighboring city. Her long brown hair was braided neatly, and Rusty thought he caught a bit of her fragrance.

"eyy! Rusty ! Wat hapen?" Duke Shook him, he flinched and stared at him.

"not...nothing" he hurried to return his eyes to Eren but she was gone.

The bell rung ,everyone hurried to thier classes like a flock hypnotized ants heading to their death traps.

Rusty and Duke sat at the back, near the window where they can entertain themselves in the middle of a boring class.

The class had settled and the teacher, Miss Mantia arrived.

"good morning class" she said beaming at them her red lips stretched beautifully on her rosy cheeks.

"good morning lovely" Duke mumbled staring at miss Mantia.

Rusty snorted, and chuckled.

"s...She's lovely isn't she"

"SHE IS !"

miss Mantia checked the attendance and started their first lesson. Mathematics.

"math is a curse of the creator,givin to torment the living" Duke complained ,hitting his pen aggressively on the desk, his eyes glued on his empty paper.

"I agree" Rusty knodded vigorously,staring at his own empty paper.

"fifteen minutes children" miss Mantia said gently, observing everyone, her long skinny neck stretched around.

Rusty scribbled illegible characters and figures.hoping miss Mantia would grade him based on determination and not on accuracy. He filled his paper with erasures and unnecessary and inaccurate arrows, points and x's.

"times up children ,papers please"miss Mantia collected the papers from one desk to another, examining their works for brief seconds.

Rusty wished she forgets about him. But Miss Mantia approached him slowly, he handed her his paper slightly trembling.

She took the paper and stared at it,

"no !,please don't!"Rusty was yelling inside his mind.

"I see that you are eager to solve the problem Mr.Luvré"she smiled at him sweetly and proceeded on Duke's work.

Duke's face was contorted just like his, his jaw was clenched, he swallowed .

"spend more effort next time Mr.Thots" Miss Mantia said looking at Duke's paper.

"yes Miss Mantia" Duke sank, Rusty tried hard to surpress a giggle.

"how did you do it?!" duke clapped Rusty's back. They were now walking out the room for break."I tried hard but I can't get the answer"

"n...nor did I"

Duke's eyes widened, a smirk grew on his lips

"you scumbag"he laughed resting his arm on Rusty's shoulder.

He-Rusty and Duke went to the caferteria.

The cafeteria was crowded with students, heads bobbing up an down holding thier trays.

Rusty and Duke lined to get their food. Behind other students Rusty saw Eren, she was talking to Leon Cleves the son of the school principal. Her smile was so warm, the fluffy creature on Rusty's stomach awoken. It brushed itself in Rusty's stomach tickling him.

Leon left coolly ,out the cafeteria. Eren joined her friends on thier table and gossiped about something.

The creature wanted Rusty to approach Eren and kiss her.

"eyyyy,Rusty they only have milk from your dairy" Duke said sheepishly pointing to the small blue boxes with thier brand logo- A barn.

"I'm not having milk today then"he said flatly, hurying to look at Eren again.

She stood up still talking to her friends, smiling. Some of her friends giggled as she brushed past through them towards to cafeteria door.

The creature wanted him to follow Eren and he obeyed.

"Duke,c...could you get my food,I need to be somewhere,"

"sure,what do you want?"

"anything, don't wait for me too"he said and hurried to follow Eren.

He zig-zaged pass the swarm of harmless but annoying students. He lost sight of Eren.

He ran to her room ,when he reached her he will hold her hand tightly or if possible hug her and soak in her flowery fragrance. His heart lept on the thought.

He reached her room, but she wasn't there, only a couple of her classmates occupied the room.

"hello russle what brou-"

"hello" he greted them without letting her finish her sentence.

He jogged, enduring the prickling pain on his hip, down the hall and out the cluster of rooms.

He marched through the field under the blazing sun, Rusty saw the sleeve of Eren's flowery shirt behind the nut tree.

He smiled ,the fluffy creature was growing restless running in circles on his stomach. The walked slowly towards the tree careful not to make any noise. His heart pounded ,his grin turned even wider, but before he could reach her, and arm slipped out of the protection of the tree. Rusty jumped back. He hid behind a Bush and sneaked ,he wanted to see them closely,maybe it was one of her friends, he thought.

He peeked through the Bush and saw Eren, her brown hair fell perfectly on her back,

Rusty moved closer ,to get a better view. He found a larger gap between the leaves that anabled him to see more clearly.

Eren was with leon, something cold was poured on Rusty, the cold sipped to his heart- freezing it, it ached like a spears of ice pricked at it at the same time.

They were sitting behind the tree eren sitting on Leon's lap. Eren and Leon are hooking up, their faces were red and sweaty with passion they both are full with,Eren's hands were resting on Leon's chest . Leon was wrapping Eren in his arms, just like Rusty did the night of the party.

The creature on his stomach gave a horrible howl, Rusty felt it's fluff hardened turning into quills, it hurted him in every breath. His chest tightened, his heart beated furiously that is seems it wanted to fly away, be far ,and never to return again.

He wanted to leave but can't, his knees were trembling and he might fall if he even dared to stand up. He can do nothing but watch. The pain struck again and again like endless waves ,only the waves weren't water but countless numbers of sharp knives.

Eren broke the kiss, smiling at leon her lips were so red and swollen, she flattened her ruffled hair and kissed leon on the cheek. Leon's smile turned into a grin. He brushed himself up and stared at Eren , then left, leaving her behind the tree, panting.

Rusty bit his tongue to stop himself from yelling. His chest pounded abnormally. His throat dried as a lump grew, he swallowed hard but the lump wouldn't go. His eyes burned ,anger and pain swirled inside him, filling his whole being.

Eren regained her breath and followed leon shortly to the cafeteria, where no one knows what happen. Only Rusty and his now dying fluffy creature.

Rusty collapsed on the ground, the grass was cold and damp, it felt like the grass was sharing his gloom. He sniffed the air, he smelled Eren's flowery fragrance, it stung his nose, it was absurd that the scent he once loved hurt him so much. He inhaled deeply and toughened his core. He pulled himself up and concealed his sadness by a wide radiant smile.

He limped as he entered the cafeteria, the pain on his hip increased greatly. He avoided to stare at anyones eyes, afraid that they might see his real situation. The chatter of the cafeteria irritated him, everyone was hitting his shoulder, shouting on his ear, gossiping with his eyes on him, giggling. He hated it. He draw a very deep breath and plastered the fakest smile he can master.

"eyyyyy,,over her"he recognised the voice as Duke

He laughed and joined him in the table.

"w...what dya got me"

Duke pointed at a small blue box with a barn logo.

"haha,funny"

"I know you won't like the others,so I figured I'll get you milk instead"

"do you have bread at least?"he said, thankful Duke haven't noticed.

"I got toast",he handed Rusty two slices of buttered toast.

"bet the butter is your product too" Duke added taking a bite of his own toast.

Rusty ate his tasteless toast and sipped the milk carton dry, keeping his thoughts away from Eren or leon or even from flowers. He attended the next classes faking his mood. His desire of the school bell grew each second, he felt tired and weak but he didn't want anyone to know. He gazed at the school yard outside the window. Suppressing a yawn, the dying sunlight was making him dizzy.

"Mr.Luvré? Are you alright?" Mrs. Dhonan, the science teacher asked him

"I...I am alright Mrs.Dhonan"

"very well,now Mr.Luvré could you tell us what is a chlorophyll?"Mrs. Dhonan eyed him sharply, clearly she noticed Rusty's unatentiveness.

"a...a chlorophyll is a pigment,a green pigment that is vital for... for photosynthesis" he answered hoping his answer is enough to satisfy her.

Mrs. Dhonan knodded and turned the other students. His answer seemed to reach Mrs.Dhonan's satisfactory ,she didn't disturbed him afterwards, the minutes passed like tortoises, Rusty was feeling so heavy he just wanted to lie down, as if faith took him pity the school bell rung ,students packed thier bags happily ,the chatter grew instantly, it grew louder each second. The noise hit Rusty like a dull axe, not enough to break him open but more than enough to cause pain.

"So last week of school isn't it? What are your plans?" Duke placed a hand on Rusty's shoulder.

"I'll be working on 'MY' factory" Rusty faked a tone of pride.

"good luck man"Duke clapped Rusty's back

"y..you?"

"ehhh" Duke shrugged his nose crumpled, "help at the bakery for sure"

"and speaking of my precious little bakery,I gotta run " Duke snatched his bag and waved good-bye before running out the room.

"bye" Rusty said to the ghost Duke left behind.

He threw his books back to his bag , he wanted to leave the room, he kept his head down, avoiding everyone's eyes, for those eyes might be Leon's or worse.... Eren's. There was no tingling in his stomach anymore, there was a hole on his chest. A hollow space inside him, that space inside him felt numb but weighed so much at the same time.

The afternoon sun was shining on the school yard, the grass glowed orange, the old cracked benches seemed warm and inviting, there was pink tinge on the pale blue skies.He inhaled deeply hoping it would help him, the warm air traveled from his nostrils down to the base of his throat into his lungs.

He found their car and hurried to climb inside.

"how are you dear?"Mrs. Luvré asked Rusty warmly,as the car moved and tackled thier way home, her radiant skin reflected the light of the dying sun.

"fine mother"Rusty smiled at her, his first sincere smile since .....

"of course you're fine boy" Mr. Luvré spat, his eyes clawing on Rusty's whole being.

"the mayor told me that you acted funny in the face of her daughter, I'm telling you..."

"it..it's her who acted funny !"

"don't you reason with me boy,I know what you did,I know you harrassed her"

"but Rusty can't do that ,can you dear?"Mrs. Luvré was looking worried

"of...of course,I can't mother "

"he is Russle Sarah!,that boy is Russle!, and he harrassed the mayor's daughter, among all people,the boy is a nitwit!"Mr. Luvré's voice roared even louder than the car's engine.

"y...yeah he got that from his father"

"how Dare y..!!"Mr. Luvré stopped the car and faced Rusty, his eyes were furious.

"I am your father ,boy" he pointed a skinny finger on Rusty

"father who?"

Mr. Luvré's furious face turned even Wilder, his eyes widened his irises shrinked, he raised a hand and slapped Rusty.

"no ! Edward !,don't hurt my son!"Mrs. Luvré cupped Rusty's redening cheek, a tear slid down her face

"behave.... yourself dear"she whispered, her eyes were watery, her voice cracky, she seemed on the brink of crying.

"fine!,side with the boy"Mr. Luvré said stiring the car.

They arrived at manor without a word, Rusty immediately darted to his room, ignoring Lucy's greetings.

He threw himself on the bed and yelled on his pillow, his muffled yells filled his room. He greeted his teeth and punched his pillow but refused to cry. His cheek was hot as if a pressing iron was shoved on his face, hot tears formed on the corners of his eye, but he blinked to stop them from flowing. How would you're great father react if he saw you crying, he mocked. He collapsed on his bed and closed his eyes, the pain lulling him to sleep.

There was a soft knock on his door.

"ple...please leave" he said, but no voice came out.

"Rusty dear ,I brought you dinner,it's late ,you should eat"Lucy entered his room. Her soapy scent cleared Rusty's lungs. She placed the dinner on his desk. She lit the oil lamp,light was showered in the room.She turned at him slowly.He looked at her trying to master a smile. Lucy return the smile but it faded immediatly, she bursted into tears, her hands on her mouth.

"ohh dear" she cried, stretching her arms for Rusty. He accepted it and burried his face on her neck.

"what happened?tell me" she asked, eyeing his red cheek.

"it...it's nothing"he said lowly

Lucy sighed and patted his back. Her warm embrace gave Rusty strength, he always saw Lucy as one of his mothers, her gentle head pats rocks him to sleep, her soapy smell soothes his mind, her overall care makes him feel..'well cared for'.

"I have to go now Rusty dear,eat your dinner"

"thanks Lucy"He let go of her keeping his face down.

"of course...of course"Rusty didn't saw her face but he knew she was smiling. Lucy left him, her soft footsteps echoed against the hard cold floor.

Rusty sat on a stool facing his desk and fed himself slowly, the food was delicious, the meat was so tender and the vegetables are crips.

Someone knocked on the door.

"Rusty,it's me"his mother said, her voice was muffled.

"c...come in mother"

The door creaked as it opened, revealing his mother in her satin night gown.

"I wanted to give you something dear,"she gupled

"ugh what's the point of lying,I wanted to see you son,"she came closer, she examined rusty's cheek with her finger on the light of the lamp.

"it stings" his mother pressed his swelling cheek too hard.

"I'm sorry ,I wanted to check on you" her eyes watered, the tears that grew at the corner of her eyes sparkled in the light.

"since I'm here"she reached for Rusty's hand, it was shiny gold ring the glow of the lamp shined three times brighter on it's surface.

"why would I want his ring?"

"it's not his,it's your brother's,I know he'll want you to have that."

"thank you mother "

His mother smiled and knodded, she stared at Rusty one more time and left the room. Rusty examined the ring, it was made of pure gold, a thin slanting "luvré" was carved on it's surface. He inserted a leather strap through it and fashioned it into a necklace, He put it on and the cold ring sat against his skin.

"he will never be like Benjamin!,my boy was so precious, he's nothing like him!" His father's voice thundered from the other room

"keep your voice down Edward please" his mother begged crying.

"that boy was a disgrace ,an ungrateful careless dumbheaded brat!" his father spat

Anger filled Rusty like poison, he snatched his backpack and poured the books inside, he grabbed some of his shirts ,trousers and even underwares, and shoved them inside his bag.

He grabbed a pen and started making his letters, one for lucy another for his mother.

Dear Lucy,

The time you are able to read this, Im off already, please take care of yourself while I'm gone.

Love, Rusty

Dear mother,

I wanted time to think and find my peace, please understand.

Love, Rusty

He shoved the letters on his pocket and waited for the right moment. He placed his stoll near the window where he can observe the nights, until he was sure his parents are asleep.

The night crept deeper, it was time, he opened his door very quietly, carrying the bag on his back, his leather boots squeaks as he steps, he dropped on his knees and slowly removed his boots, he left it at his door. He slowly crept to his parent's bedroom, he opened the door slowly, the room was dead quiet, only his father's snores are heard, his mother was facing the window her back at him, her shoulders rises and falls with her breath. The light of the moon outside shined on the window, it's light scattered on the desk beside the table where his father's wallet sat, he immediately grabbed it and replaced it with his letter. The wallet was thick with bills, he shoved it inside his bag's pocket. Rusty glanced at the figure of his sleeping mother and sighed then turned, he left the room without a single noise.

With large steps he barefootedly returned to his room to pick up his boots . He didn't put it on but instead carried it on his hands.he descended the stairs and turned towards the kitchen, he placed his letter above the stove and left the Manor through the kitchen door.

Rusty haistely put on his boots and tackled the dirtroad to the town, walking at night seemed easier than at day, there is no Sweat nor there is sticky humid air. The dirt road is much easier to follow now that he had been here. It took him almost an hour to reach the town.

The town was different from Rusty had remembered it, the shops are closed and there are no carriages on the road. He noticed train tracks hidden behind the series of shops. He jogged following the tracks and found himself in a small old train station. A high pitch whistle of an incoming train traveled through the night air. From a distance a single bright light was coming, the tracks was shaking and the rowing of wheels intensified.

A large black train halted in front of Rusty, steam covered the station floor as if the train had come down from heaven. Rusty climbed the train and found a few passegengers already inside.

"which station are you lad?" a stubby man with a goaty asked him, smiling with his dented front teeth.

"how far could you get me?"

"the farthest?, well,this train reaches the coast of Mortiana "

"take me there"

"alrighty then"the man gave Rusty ticket, the paper was dirty gray in colour.

Rusty paid him and find himself a seat. He sat on a vacant seat on the right window of the train, he layed his head against the cold glass, it soothed his swelling cheek, he smiled and closed his eyes, as the train rowed it's wheel faster and farther.

CHAPTER 4

"Hey lad,open those lazy eyes and hop off"

Rusty woke up with a start, his eyes wandered around the train. The seats were vacant, there are no passengers left.

"we're here"the man flicked his head to the window. Dawn was set low on the horizon, the ground was black and the sky orangy.

"th...thanks"

Rusty pulled his bag up to his shoulder and and bowed to the man. He hopped off the train. The chill kissed his skin, he was standing in a small old station, it is still dark but Rusty can see that the bricks of the station are old and ragged. He inhaled deeply the cold air, and Shook himself. It's too early, Mortiana is still asleep. There was a row of benches leaning against the station's wall, the bench creaked as he slumped on it. He stayed motionless, his eyes closed, the cold breeze wrapped him, and slowly sipped into his bones.

Rusty's jaw rattled uncontrollably, he hugged his bag tight and burried his face on it. He slowly fell into a shallow dreamless sleep.

Morning came, the sun warmed up the air, a lone sunbeam played on Rusty's forehead. Rusty woke up, dazzled by the lights. He stretched and yawned. People that passed threw him dirty

looks, his hair was so untidy. Like he had faced a storm unshield-
ed.

A police officer wearing a navy blue shirt and trousers patrolled the station, his eyes were suspicious,lines stretched on his fore-head, his brows soaring. He calmly approached Rusty, Rusty saw him and immediately straightened on his bench , rubbing his eyes.

"good morning there young man"

"good morning officer" Rusty bowed suppressing another yawn.

"are you waiting for train?"

"oh no,I arrived here too early ,I figured I'll wait the morning here"

"is that so?,"

Rusty knodded truthfully

"is there someone to pick you up?"

"no...no there isn't"

The officer's brow collided, he struck Rusty a heavy look.

"is there a place I can stay here officer?" he hurried to change the subject, the lines on the officer's forehead disappeared.

"theres the inn but it's always full, there is a cluster of cabins near the shore too,just ask around for Rowlin,"

"thanks...thanks officer"

The officer knodded and strolled away, a small silver gun was peeking trough his back pocket.

Rusty pulled his bag and started on his way to town. The town of Mortiana was just as busy as his.People, both young and old walked the streets, Although there were less cars, and carriages were older and much more 'rickety'.Cobbled streets were laid throughout the town, houses stack on top of one another forming a towering structure.

"excuse me ma'am,I am looking for Rowlin,do you know where I can find her?" He asked a woman with a droopy nose and watery eyes.

"go to the cabins near the shore,you will find HIM there"the woman stressed the word him, beaming at Rusty.

"thank you"

Rusty reached the shore, the air was salty, the sound of waves are carried by the wind, the sand muffled his step. The sky and sea was shining on blues. The clouds above are white thick, moving like an army of sheeps soaring on the skies.

He knocked on the biggest cabin,the cabin was tall its windows are thick glass ,a tall brick chimney poked out the roof.

A beefy man with a strong jaw opened the door, his wide shoulders barely fit on the door gap, his hair was long ,dry and red.

"good morning I ...I am looking for Rowlin"

A feline smile appeared on the man's face. Making him look like a dressed lion.

"that would be me you are looking for, and who could you be?,"

"I'm Rusty"

"hello rusty, pleased to make your acquaintance,how could I help?" he offered Rusty a large hand, Rusty Shook it briefly.

"I'm looking for a place to stay,a nice officer earlier said you might have a cabin"

"surely!," Rowlin's smile grew larger, he moved aside ,unlocking the door.

"please ,please come in"

Rusty entered his cabin,thick dark carpets and wood furnitures gave life to the cabins yellowish wooden wall, light from the sun outside speared through the thick glass windows hitting the reddish waxed floor that shined under it. Mixed scents of liquor and tea caught Rusty's nose.

"I have to thank the good officer" Rowlin pulled a small stool and motioned Rusty to sit.

"the cabins outside" he glanced outside the window.

"I wa...want the cheapest cabin"

Rowlin laughed holding his stomach.

"my cabins are cheap young man"

"Im staying alone,can you lower the price?"

Rowlin stopped his giggling and scanned Rusty up and down.

"you're such a fine lad young Rusty, someone like shouldn't be alone,you are young afterall"

"I'm...I'm fourteen"

Rowlin chuckled softly, shaking his lowered head, a hand on his chin.

"of course you are,let me show you your cabin then"

Rowlin rested his hand on Rusty's shoulder, he maneuvered both of them into the cabin nearest to the shore, it's was a small cabin, very small. The lined wooden walls are blackened with time, it's door is narrow and shabby looking, the roof was missing few of it's tiles.

"it's the cheapest I got,you can even pay it by working part time in the inn"

"I'll take it"Rusty said, his hair swaying in the blow of the ocean breeze.

Rowlin opened a palm, holding it out for Rusty, Rusty rummaged through his father's wallet and pulled out a blue bill called trion. Rowlin's brown eyes widened.

"oh lad ,ten shellies would be enough"

Rusty shoved his hands on his pocket, searching for his own money, he handed Rowlin nine gold shellies and ten silver bonells. Rowlin accepted it and burried it deep in his dusty pocket.

"let me help you get inside then" he opened the door for Rusty. The cabin, wasn't shabby at all in the inside, a lamp sat on a shiny desk ,a velvet cushion sat beside it on one corner, a small bed was placed under a window.

The small cabin has an even smaller kitchen. A stove was placed above a stone floor .

"you have to get yourself wood to cook tho,but you can always swing by the inn to eat"Rowlin smiled at him before leaving closing the door behind him with a loud bang.

Rusty threw his backpack on the bed and gazed at the window.

The sea was calm, small slow maves hit the shore like curtains of winds. The sand pale beige in colour layed untouched, keeping a smooth flat surface, few birds soar the skies riding on the breeze, dancing to a silent tune only they can understand. The sun was covered in thick cotton clouds that had glued themselves against the sapphire blue skies like snowy mountains floating on the sea.

Rusty felt sticky and worn-out, a bathroom door stood ajar beside the kitchen, he walked in and freshened himself. The water was soothing and warm,

"this cabin is great"he said, drying his hair with a towel.

His stomach rumbled like a growling puny monster. He checked the kitchen cupboard but it was empty. He still need wood if he dared to cook. Rusty pulled on a pair of trousers and a shirt from his bag, he dressed himself and laced his boots snugly. He shoved his father's wallet in his pocket and marched out his cabin. He took in the salty air. His chest rising slowly, he passed the cluster of cabins and ended up in a cobbled street, no carts or people walked to and fro the streets,a small garden bed adorned the side of the road, tall bushes with lilac flowers grew on it, the flowers reminded him the dress Eren wore at the night of the party. The void in his chest came to existence suddenly, but the pain was now nothing but a dull prick on his heart, a swelling sensation grew on his chest, like a ballon had been inflated inside his lungs. He Shook off the sensations and mentally punched himself, invisioning two versions of himself one was coiled in a circle lying on the ground one in rage bombarding the other with punches and kicks.

He followed the empty street and ignored to lilac flowers that lined it's side. Houses begun to spawn on the side and the flowers disappeared, he googled the first house he layed his eyes into, it was an averagely large house metal railings stood infront of the door a lamp sprouts just above it, the bricks of the walls are cracked, it was a towering structure, its windows are noticably dusty. Rusty advanced ,his head in constant movement at the sight . He reached a busier street, carriages pulled by mules and horses alike dashed from four directions. Women in shabby blouses and aprons walked side-by-side the darknened pavement. They were clutching each other's arms, gossiping with one hand holding a basket. Rusty saw a structure made of shiny yellowish wood it's roof was lined with red tiles ,people on the inside are visible through the large glass window. A menu was posted outside show-ing the day's meals. He pushed the door open and the a mixture of diffrent herbs and sauces overwhelmed his nose.

"Rusty ! There you are "Rowlin's voice rose above everyone's. He was carrying a filthy sack on his arms ,he smiled at him, and disappeared through the kitchen door.

Rusty smiled and knodded at him,he felt himself shrink ap-parently Rowlin had took the liberty to announce his arrival. He hated the stares.

"hello there young sir,care to check the menu?" a short old man approachcd him, his red face show no sign of enthusiasm as he asked.

"yes please"

The man sighed lowly and gave Rusty a crumpled piece of hard paper.

"we have discount for scallops today would you like to try?" he asked flatly.

"oh no thank you,I'll have a ham sandwich"

"please wait for your ham sandwich"the man said, mumbling what sounded like "city people" and "seafood hater" as he returned to the counter.

Rusty gazed out the window, a fat woman was heading her way to the inn's entrance a frail girl with curly waistlength hair tailed behind her .

"here's your ham sandwich sir,that would be two boneels and two suds"said the man, his voice was glumpier than earlier.

Rusty reached for his pocket and paid the man three silver bonnels, the man reached for his pocket too and gave Rusty eight bronze suds for change.

"th...thanks" Rusty mumbled and the man grunted before turning his back against him. Rusty took a bite of his sandwich, the bread was bland but moist, the luttuce isn't fresh but the ham is great. He chewed slowly, his thoughts traveling back to the Manor, his father would be furious but he didn't care, Lucy and his mother must be worried, he stopped chewing at the thought ,a small lump formed in his throat ,"I'm sure they will understand"he reassured himself and swallowed painfully, his throat seemed to narrowed.

There was a loud bang ,rusty flicked his head to the door. The fat woman came in,her bright yellow dress and frizzy bushy black hair made her look like a miscolored dandelion fluff.

"where's Rowlin?,give me Rowlin"she shouted, her yellowish teeth showing contrasted on her bright red lipstick .

Rowlin bursted out the kitchen door his sleeves were rolled up his shoulder, his wild hair tied back on his head, beads of sweat sparkled on his forehead.

"Thildy!,hello,how nice of you to visit"Rowlin greeted her, moving closer to her.

"no ,stay away,you smell like garlic," Thildy pushed him away with her stubby fingers.

"I won't pay you a visit, if you haven't forgot what today is" Thildy said, pushing her chin up like a fat yellow Peacock.

"of course,of course,I know what today is,please Thildy let's talk somewhere else"Rowlin motioned the inn's back door. "let the girl eat while we talk"

"no ,the girl won't have anything,she don't have a single sud"Thildy said, without paying the girl any look.

Thildy walked rather too slowly towards the back door, Rowlin tailed behind her. He closed the door soflty and they vanished from everyone's eyes.

The girl stood alone at the door, her frail hands swung grimly on her sides. Her eyes jumps on everyone's food until they reached the sandwich on Rusty's hands. There eyes met and the girl looked away hurriedly trying to burry herself on the wall even deeper.

Rusty stood up from his seat and walked to the counter. His steps was slow and steady, he felt the girls eyes following him.

"could I have another ham sandwich?"he asked the man.

"of course sir"the man said turning to prepare his order.

"and tw...two drinks as well"

"we only have orange juice sir"

"that would do,thanks"

"that would be three boneels and two suds"the man said, his eyes fixing on Rusty for the first time. Rusty dugged his pocket and paid the man.

"thank you my good sir,please wait at your table"

Rusty returned to his table, he didn't touched his sandwich but secretly stared at the girl, her black hair darkened even more under the shadow, her stained dress was ruffled and creases stretched on unnatural places.

"there you go sir"the man said placing two glasses of orange juice and a new fresh sandwich. He left without another word.

Rusty stared at the girl, she haven't moved a spot, he walked towards her keeping a steady pace to avoid setting off the girl. Her eyes were fixed on the floor staring at her feet.

"hello, would you like to join me at my table?"he asked politely, his voice lowered so that only the girl could hear.

"I dont need your pity"the girl murmured her head sank even lower.

"I...I dont pity you"He lied"I don't like to be pitied as well,that's why I'm asking you to eat with me,that way I won't be alone looking like a cast-out"

"I'm not hungry"she said but her stomach disagreed it rumbled loudly, her ears turned red.

Rusty chuckled lowly"I know you're not, please pretent you're enjoying your food"he grabbed the girl's hand . The girl followed him limply she must have drained out of energy. He pulled a seat and offered it to her. She sat opposite to Rusty.

"go on"he offered her the sandwich and juice, she took it and pushed the sandwhich to her mouth. Rusty observed her as she eat. She chewed gracefully, her lips were pursed and her jaw moved slowly, making no sound. She pulled back her long black hair behind her ear and sipped the juice, her pink lips kissingthe glass's brim.

"could I eat without you looking at me" she asked without staring at him.

"oh sorry" Rusty chuckled taking a bite on his own sandwich.

"thanks"he said smiling at her.

She looked at him, her eyes were bright brown with flecks of gold. Her lips stayed pursed. She shrugged and continued to eat her sandwich.

Rusty resumed on his and they ate in total silence , the people in the inn started to thin out, the old man wiped the tables and cleaned the floor everytime someone leaves.

"yes Rowlin! I'm giving you a month,this is your last chance,you better have that fifteen trions or the local police will come to pick you!" Thildy's voice roared outside the inn's back door. The girl immediately stood up, wiped her lips with the back of her hand and ran back to the wall. Sinking herself in it's surface

"but Thildy that's only thirteen trions" Rowlin protested opening the door. His face had lost colour ,his lips were pale and dry.

"I said fifteen, then fifteen it would be -where is that girl?,those two trions are for my kindness"she searched for the girl and pulled her by the arm "not everyone will have the understanding like mine, to give you another month, be sure that you will have my full fifteen trions Rowlin" she pointed a stubby finger on Rowlin's chest and stabbed him three times with it. The girl hang limply on her other arm. She pulled her out the inn and the door closed with a bang. Rowlin sighed and pinched the bridge of his nose. He inhaled hard ,shaking his body, moments after he was looking much livelier.

Rusty witdrawed his stare and pretended to be invested on his empty glass like a mildly interesting book.

"you okay there Rusty?"Rowlin asked,beaming at him his voice was high as if nothing happened

"yeah"he replied waving at Rowlin as he entered the kitchen door.

He stood up and wiped off the non existent crumbs on his chest and trousers. He left the inn noiselessly and walked down the Cobbled streets ,his lunch should've been delicious, if not for Thildy, her proud movements and the way she talked with Rowlin reminded Rusty of his father, he hated her.

CHAPTER 5

Rusty was walking down a particularly old street of the town. His head straight, hands in his pockets he stopped and idly stared at the late afternoon sky and sighed, not that sighing can really do anything, he just wanted to. The sky was clear like a vast sea. The small summer sun shone brightly, dazzling him, he covered his eyes with the back of his hands and blinked hard, darkspots appeared on his sight. He continued walking until he reached a cluster of buildings different from the houses of the town, the buildings doesn't stack on top of one another but stick closely side by side, like large roofed train compartments. Iron fences stood at the edge of the lot, incasing the buildings inside.

A bell rung, students came strolling out of the buildings carrying leather bags. Rusty saw the girl amongst the students, her black hair was braided loosely with a satin ribbon. Her head was lowered, her shoulders tensed, her gaze was glued on the ground, her steps was fast as she clutched her bag with her thin arms.

Rusty run and followed her, he bumped on the shoulders of the other students as he sweep pass them. The girl was walking funny, she appears to avoid close contact with others like they carry a contagious disease.

"hey" he said gently tapping her shoulder.

The girl jumped and looked at him sharply. She scanned him for seconds barely moving, she let out a big exhale when she remembered him.

"so you study here,isn't it summer break yet?"he asked beaming at her.

The girl stared at him blanky with her brown eyes, flecks of gold reflected the afternoon light. She grunted and pulled her lip downward.She turned her back against him. Rusty scratched his nape, embarrassment growing inside him.

"I'm Rusty by the way"he stuck out a hand to the girls back. The girl's shoulders fell as she let out a sigh. She turned around and stared at the hand with a hint of distaste, then stared at Rusty with equal force.

"what's your name?"

"Dianne"the girl answered flatly. She immediately turned her back against Rusty and walked away without paying him another look.

Rusty stared at her as her figure took a turn behind the houses and melted with the figures of others. His hand still aloft. Rusty chuckled and scrathed his nape ,shaking his head.

He shoved his hands on his pockets and started for the busy part of the town. His back against the afternoon sun that made his shadow look like a sinister being with overly long limbs. There were various noises. There were ladies gossiping in one corner, their bodies leaning on the old brick wall of a house. Children laughing arm in arm, others talking about summer break. Wheels of a creaky carriage pulled by time worn horse with chesnut hair. He barely even heard the clank of his boots which was usually noisy especially on hard ground under the loud noise of the town.

The structures were old but proud, their high roof was raising to the sky, their dark bricked walls stand strongly. Old lamposts lined the streets, the metals are eaten by Rust, turning it's smooth shiny surface into a brownish filth.

Rusty came by a small shop. A large sign was painted above it's glass door that says "Tony's grocery"a large glass window was situated on it's front side, Rusty peered inside. It was dark he can't make out the shop's inside. He pushed the door open. A bell chimed as the door opened. The shop was dark, there were aisles that lined impeccably neat,the first aisle contain packed candies, a blanket of dust was layered on it's packaging turning the pink plastic into gray. The aisles behind the first was too dark, only the outlines of the metal bars are visible.

The air inside the shop was heavy ,cold but numb, it filled Rusty's lungs like death. A subtle smell of bleach rises from the tiled floor. Small pieces of teared paper was scattered on the corners.

"what do you want?" a man rised from the counter hidden on a dark corner. His voice growly and demanding. His eyes, pale gray like storm clouds ,he stared at rusty blindly with sinister sparkle. The man was short, he had dark hair that blends in with the shadows of the shop. There were numerous scars on his dark arm.

"I...I want a...I want a basket" he stuttered, the mans stares hints that he wanted to snap Rusty into two pieces.

"three boneels"the man growled knodding to a stack of moldy grass stalk baskets stacked near the counter.

Rusty gulped and slowly reached for a basket, it smelled like damp rotting grass, he placed three silver boneels on the counter, flinching in every sound he made.

"do you...do you have veg..vegetables?"he asked , his stare actually on train poster behind the man.

"in the front window,help yourself they're cheap"the man flicked his head motioning to the only well lit part of the shop, his voice was so dry and rough like he was actually using all his strength to talk, Rusty's knees rattled as he made his way into the vegetables.

The vegetables wasn't really fresh, Rusty grabbed a limpy stalk of celery and layed in it on his basket, a couple of large pale carrots, and a large onion bulb. His hands landed on a rotting onion leaving a potent stench on it.

He was gagging, the spicy smell ran up his nose ,he can taste the rotted onion at the base of his tounge. A tear formed at the corner of his eye. He choked and coughed, breathing heavily.

The door bell chimed. Rusty stared blindly through the aisles, he listened carefully,the door closed silently, the click of the knob traveled through the dark shop,and a soft pair of footsteps advanced rhythmically.

"hi willy"a female voice greeted energetically.

Theres was low rumbling, and Rusty could tell the man was saying something, only it was too low and too growly to understand from afar.

"I brought you fish"

The man chuckled distinctly, his chuckle cracks every second like a falling tree.

"thanks ,I have to leave now"

The bell chimed again and the door closed, this time louder, faster.

Rusty clutched his basket tighly and slithered between the aisles carefull not the touch the dusty pruducts on it. The air of the shop was hugging him, squeezing him tighter with his every breath, Sweat had formed on his forehead and the tip of his nose. He bit his lips and swallowed. His boots clanked as he move toward the counter. The man which he assumed was willy was waiting for him. Half hidden in the shadows. The bridge of his nose was poking through the light. His eyes were sparkling like fragments of a broken mirror.

Rusty placed his basket on the counter. Willy stared at him and at the basket but said nothing. He raised his dark scarred arm. A wave of fear enveloped rusty, expecting willy to choke him anytime he make one wrong move.

Willy's hand slithered into the basket's rim. He pulled the basket closer to him, Rusty breathe sharply. Pinching his thigh. Willy peered inside the basket and counted the vegetables.

"two boneels ,seven suds" he pushed the basket back to Rusty.

Rusty dug out his pocket searching for coins. He gave willy three silver boneels, Willy picked the coins up, the cash register dingcd, willy pulled out three bronze suds and pushed it back to rusty.

He pocketed the coins and turned his back to Willy gripping his grass basket tightly. He can fell willys eyes following him . He almost ran when he saw the door. He pulled the knob a bit too strong, the bell chime echoed on the shop. Rusty's heart sank, he slid out the door quickly and ran, he joined the people on the street, the crowd made him fell that he was protected. He felt more bigger.

He followed the flow of people, leading him into the common part of the town, a road that leads to the inn stretched in front of him. The soft sea breeze played on his hair. The sea air warmed his lungs. He can taste the salt at the base of his tounge. He followed the old road and reached the inn. It was red under the rays the dimming sun. The glass windows reflect the waves on the beach. The inn was almost empty, only the old man was inside, polishing his counter.

He walked pass the inn, swaying his basket lightly, the road sloped down into the cluster of cabins beside the sea. Rusty grimaced at the sight. The sky was painted orange and gold behind the red setting sun, clouds stretched thinly above like silver threads. Sea birds squaked ,dancing from afar, their silhouettes appeared as black figures like shadows playing with a candle's flame.

He descended a stone stairwell that brought him to the cluster of cabins. Rowlins chimney was smoking, his dishes were clanking from the inside. He slowly walked toward his own cabin. His steps muffled by the dark sand.

"eyy Rusty !,what ya got there ?"rowlin poked his feline head out his window, smirking at Rusty.

"uh ...I...I got vegetables" Rusty smiled and jerked his shoulder.

"finally decided to cook your own food huh?"

"yes" he knodded, smirking. " I got to go,I don't have firewood"he waved his hand at Rowlin and continued walking.

"there's not a lot of drift wood here,you have to walk a bit father along the shore to find 'em" Rowlin shouted before pulling his head back.

Rusty yanked his door open, a wave of silence greeted him, the wood perfumed air inside his cabin was warm, shadows was casted on his walls, but his window, the one facing the sea was glowing. He placed his basket on the small table . He sat on his bed and sniffed, he stared at his basket, he could make vegetable stew for tonight, he stared at the kitchen, pots and pans hang neatly, a small variety of ladles were hanged beside the large pot. He still need wood.

He unlaced his boots and removed his socks. He was going to the beach and gather wood.

The sand was warm under his soles, the sand closer to the beach was finer and lighter in colour, dry tall grass grew at the side of the beach. It reminded Rusty the tall grass on the edge of the yellow field. The waves crashed on the shore like a silent storm, breeze kissed him.

He walked the edge of the beach tracing the shore, the sun casted elongated shadows againts the brown sand. There was a shiny branch that layed on the beach, waves crashed on it. He picked it up, the branch was smooth cold and damp. It was weightless. He dragged the branch by the hand. It left absurd lines on the sand.

He picked up another branch, it was gnarly and rough, but it was completely dry. He picked up another, and another, and another after that.

He was carrying his firewood on his arms. The sun had set lower, the skies were red and dark, stars appeared above the dying light. The sea stretched into a dark plain, melting and combining with the darkening sky in the horizon. The dry grass on the beach had thinned out.

Rusty noticed a cabin far away,it was dark, old, rustic. The light of the sun painted one of it's wall red. It was smaller than his, but a makeshift peir connects it to the deeper part of the sea,the slow waves played on the wooden poles on the water. Fences sorounded the small old cabin, fish nets hanged on the fences like spider webs.

Rusty walked closer.He never reached this part of mortiana, a soft breeze blew, the dry grass swayed and rustled like the clicking of the pincers of a thousand spiders. He sneaked not wanting to gather attention as he approached the fence. Cluthing the driftwoods on his arms. He streached his head to observe an open window, the cabin was utterly empty, no furniture was visible through the gap of the small window.

Rusty crept closer, entering an old wooden gate. There was a soft humming, the song was calm yet oddly bone rattling, like a siren was singing her song to lure men to their watery deaths. The humming was coming from the back of the cabin, Rusty peeked. A girl was sitting at the edge of the pier, a white satin ribbon tied back her curly black hair.

Another breeze blew. Her sirenish voice was carried by the wind, it echoed on Rusty's ear, luring him, he slowly approached her.

The pier creaked on his first step. The girl jumped, scanning him with suspecting eyes. Her high brows slowly fell but her bright brown eyes remained sharp.

"D...Dianne ?" Rusty let out a soft chuckle,

"you?" Dianne's eyes narrowed, unable to believe it was him. "what are you doing here?"

"I...i was collecting firewood"

"get your firewood and leave" Dianne waved her hand dismissively on the air before turning her back to rusty.

"you ,what are you doing here?"

Dianne stayed quite, a soft wave crashed against the pier, sea water splashed on Rusty's feet, it was warm like the sun was in his soles. A breeze followed, the salty air pushed through his lungs.

Dianne sighed her shoulders droop down,

"I live here"she said lowly. Pulling a net from the water. The net wiggled and shivered,a few couple of fishes were trapped on the nylon net, their scales sparkled like metal on the red sunlight. Dianne plucked the fishes out . She picked the larger ones and threw in a bucket,and placed the smaller ones in another bucket.

"wh...why do you seperate the fishes?, they're all the same. They're still fishes"

" I sell the larger ones "

"and the small ones?"

"they're dinner,so please leave me alone" Dianne picked up her buckets and walked pass rusty, the scent of her hair reached Rusty's nose above the salty scent of the fish and sea, it smelled like fresh grass and wild flowers.

"Dianne wait" Rusty stretched his hand to help her with the bucket.

Dianne looked back and struck him with a sharp look, she pulled her shoulder and walked toward her own cabin.

"get your firewood and leave" she said wihout turning back.

Rusty followed her but a part of the peir snapped off, Rusty's heart raced, a searing pain bit his leg, salt intensified the pain, his lower torso fell and scratched against the pier floor,the skin on his stomach stung , he clinged on to the planks,the pain on his lower body merge into one giant unpointable pain.

"help!"he screamed gritting his teeth, the salty water wasn't doing him any favor.

Dianne rushed toward him, her eyes wide in shock, her hand trembled as she reached for him, she pulled him out, her frail arms managed to tug him out from the bite of the pier floor.

"what happened" she asked, voice shaky, she examined him with trembling hands.

"the floor..... The floor......snapped.....off" he grunted, blood was oozing through his trousers. He wheezed when the wound stung even more when a breeze hit it.

"can you walk?"

"I...I guess " he pushed him self up, the pain was growing, it reached his lower knee, he failed on his first step and fell on the floor.

Dianne wrapped her arms around his waist and pulled him up, Rusty clung on her shoulder. He limped as Dianne carried her to her cabin.

She placed him on a low stool .Rusty grunted as he rested his back against the cabin wall.

"we need to wash it" she said without pause and ran to scoop up water from a Clay jug into a small basin. She carried the basin to Rusty.

Dianne folded back his trouser, she clapped a hand on her mouth, her eyes wide.

"is...is...it that bad?" Rusty asked, his breathing was labored and heavy ,

"your....you're skin had peeled off " she said, eyeing his injured leg.

Dianne gently run his leg with water.

"awww......it stings" he sniffed, the pain reacted on the base of his head, a tear slid down his cheek, beads of Sweat formed on his forehead.

"I know,Im trying to do it quick"

Rusty bit his lip, and moaned, balling his fists. The pain came to him aggressively, his whole body bacame numb ,his head became light, he felt dizzy, but the pain on his leg remained active, it pulsed and Stung.

"please hurry" he cried, tears flowing out his eye.

"there, its done" she said finally.

Rusty stared at his leg, a large piece of skin flapped out his calf, his flesh was so pale, bruise had formed around his open flesh, a long slit run down from his lower calf to his ankle.

"would you cut it off?" he asked staring at the hanging piece of skin.

"no," Dianne ripped out a blanket into strips, she aligned the skin into the flesh and started wrapping his leg.

"I suppose you can't walk your way home tonight?" she asked, but her eyes was calm, Rusty can see the sincerity on it.

"I....I'm sorry"

"fine, stay here for a while" she tapped his leg gently and stood up "I need your wood"

"oh....I left them near the gate" he said taking effort to keep his voice from shaking.

Dianne left him ,her soft footsteps echoed on the growing night's air. She returned carrying the wood on her arms. She gently placed it down under a fireplace and searched for her pocket, Dianne pulled out a box of matches. She silently made a fire, Rusty watched her do it, the pain on his leg had decreased into a tolerable state when Dianne had covered it up, it pulsed as the blood circulated on his leg.

Dianne blew on the fire, it roared to life, light had scattered into the cabin, it wasnt moldy as it looked on the outside, it's walls are well cleaned, the floor was shiny . Not an abundant number of ornaments are inside the cabin, only a small chest with metal frames, a small wooden table and a small old cabinet sits against a wall

Dianne picked up a large fish and started cleaning it. She rinsed it with water and started scaling it with a knife. She cut the fish's head and chopped the body into four. She rinsed it again and put it in a blackened metal pot. Dianne noiselessly carried the pot and hanged it inside the fireplace.

"stay here" she muttered, Rusty knodded at her, without even knowing what she'll do.

Dianne opened the cabin door and glided outside her black hair dancing with the wind. Rusty watched as her figure slowly become one with the dark night.

Rusty sighed and looked at his leg, he can feel the open flesh underneath the thick wrapping. He ran a hand trough it, gently pressing his skin, the wound grew very painful at the slightest touch. He sniffed ,locking his jaw.

The cabin door burst open, and Dianne came in, a cluster of big leaves in her hands, the leaves were dark green, it's shiny surface reflected the honey light of the fire. Rusty stared at Dianne.

"it's for your wound" she said, and placed the damp leaves beside rusty.

Dianne filled another pot with water and carried it to the fire,she kneeled, crouching to hang the pot on the low fireplace, the fire twirled and tickled the bottom of the pot, Dianne's eyes burned as she stares at it, the fire reflected on her eyes sparkled like a cluster of stars.

Dianne stood up, brushing her shabby skirt. She turned to Rusty and picked up the leaves.

"how's your leg?"

"painful" Rusty answered truthfully, he gave Dianne a reassuring smile. "nothing I can't handle"

Dianne scoofed and turned to the pot, "of course,nothing you can't handle" she murmured.

She placed the leaves on the pot and started stirring it. The pot gave off an odd scent . It was like fresh trimmed grass with a hint of bitterness. Dianne checked her stewed fish. She stood up and walked towards the small cabinet. She pulled out a couple of bowls and spoons, Dianne placed it on the table. She walked back to Rusty.

"let's have dinner" she wrapped her arms on his waist. Her skin was warm through his shirt. Rusty straightened and limped with her toward the table.

Dianne helped him settle on a small wooden chair before turning back on the fireplace ,she kneeled ,covered her hand with a piece of fabric and took off the fish stew ,she carefully held the hot pot on her hands and placed it on the table.

She laddled and serve Rusty the fish stew. The bowl was steaming, it's fragrant smell tickled Rusty's nose. He patiently waited until Dianne was done on hers.

She drained the pot and placed it on a sink, before joining Rusty.

"where are your parents ?,it's late ,aren't they supposed to be home?" he asked, laying his eyes on Dianne.

Dianne stared back at him, "they're not coming"

"why"

"my mother died giving birth to me" Dianne said, her head low.

A lump grew on Rusty's throat ,he casted Dianne an apologitic look, he hesitated but asked anyway "and your father?"

"he went fishing one night,but a storm popped up all of a sudden,he never came back" Dianne said with firm and clear voice, but Rusty saw her swallow, a tear also appeared at the corner of her eye.

"I...I'm sorry" Rusty said below his breath

"it's fine ,I'm fine"Dianne smiled and spooned out her stew.

Rusty spooned out his own, they ate quietly but he secretly observes Dianne.

"you ?,why are you here?,your family must miss you greatly"

"I ran away" Rusty raised his shoulders

Dianne stared at him for a short second, her eyes glowing against the flame. Rusty continued to sip his stew.

When dinner was done Dianne gathered the dishes and placed them in the sink. She helped Rusty clean up his face, wiping a damp cotton on his cheeks.

"lets wash your wound again"she said. Taking the pot off the fireplace, she poured the boiled leaves on a basin. Steam was coming out from the greenish water. Dianne unwrapped his leg carefully, the old fabric strips became red with his blood, the smell of iron is potent. She finished unwrapping the whole leg, his leg was a bright shade of red, the bruising had calm down, but the slit on his ankle is swelling .

Dianne slowly trickled the hot water on his wound. Rusty gritted his teeth, his eye brows crossed. She used a damp cloth to wipe his wound. It was painful at first but the warm water had soothed his leg. Dianne wiped all the hardened blood off. She took one of the leaves off the water and covered the wound with it.

"why?" rusty asked her, his eyes on the leaf.

"your skin would stick to the fabric when I cover it.the leaf will help avoid that."she answered wrapping his leg with fresh frabric sheets.

She carried the basin to the sink . Then walked toward the chest.

"you should get ready for sleep"she said while rummaging in her metal framed chest. She pulled out an old pair of tattered trousers and a long sleeve shirt. She handed it to Rusty. "go change"

Dianne turned around as Rusty began to strip, he put on the shirt and carefully removed his trousers, he placed his old clothes in a chair, Rusty pulled on the tattered trouser, it was cool against his skin, it was light but comfy.

"here" Dianne patted a spot on the floor in front of the fire place. She covered it with a woolen blanket, a pair of pillows above it.

Rusty hopped on one foot to Dianne, he slowly sat on the floor,grunting as he did so. He layed his head on the pillow. The smelled like lemon,relaxing and calm,he sniffed the air comfortably catching the scent.Dianne layed on the pillow next to him,her skin was glowing on the light of the fire,she burried her head deeper on her own pillow,her eyes closed.

"Dianne?" he asked the fireplace.

"hmmm?"

"we're now friends right?"

"hmmm."

Rusty smiled and rubbed his back on the floor trying to get more comfortable. The floor was hard, but he can't complain, the woolen blanket on their backs was warm and soft.

CHAPTER 6

"Dianne" The door of Dianne's cabin bursted open, Rusty came in, his face radiant as a young sun, Dianne looked at him, smiling.

"how's your leg doing ?" she asked scanning Rusty's leg through his trouser.

"it's fine,"he smiled at her ,

A week ago, Rusty fell on the pier, he injured his leg and had to spend the night on Dianne's cabin. Maybe it was not that of a bad thing really. Rusty thought, staring at Dianne's back. Her black hair danced with the breeze from the open window like waves crashing on the shore.

Something brushed against the skin of his stomach, it was fluffy. It was tickling him that he can't stop himself from smiling. His heart raised beats, it pops inside his chest, wanting to get noticed. He Shook his head and breath slowly, taking in the morning air, and letting it out slowly.

"Rusty ,are you okay?" Dianne asked him, her brown eyes met his ,the gold flecks shining on the light. The beating of his heart increased, Dianne's skin was pale but her cheeks are rosy. Few strands of her hair fell down on her nose. Her red lips ,red as a dying sun strectched into a worried look.

"Rusty?"

He Shook his head and smiled, "totally fine,yes" his eyed shrinked into slits.

Dianne wrinkled her nose, her brows crossing, she turn her back to him, and kneeled in front of a pair of old buckets, it's brims are scratched, the iron isn't shiny anymore.

"whom the fish for?" he peeked on the bucket, slowly kneeling behind her, her hair gave off a flowery fragrance, it smelled like wild flowers and ferns.

"for a friend"

"ill co...come with you"

Dianne shrugged and got up. She carried the buckets up toward the door.

"let me g..." Rusty pulled one bucket off Dianne's hands, she gave it to him with a smile. They both headed to the door, Rusty on the lead. Dianne pushed the door closed as Rusty wait for her.

They walked the beach leaving thier trail in the sand. It was a clear bright day, the sky was vivid blue, clouds are thick and white, the sun in the East was shining gold, sun beams hit them, the light played on their faces, the breeze kissed them, it made Dianne's dress flap, her cream dress played with the wind like sails of a mighty ship. Her hair bouncing in all directions, slapping Rusty playfully.

The shore was deserted, no one was playing by the beach, only the smooth pale brown sand and a few small branches.

They reached a stone stairway ,they climbed in, Rusty on Dianne's back, the stairs had blackencd over time, moss grew on it's side turning the surface green. The stair led into a cobble stone path.

The path was leading into the pier, large boats lined .bobbing up and down as the calm waves hit them, the boats were rocked to sleep the by the sea. Sea birds landed on the stone pier, squacking everytime another bird lands.

"here" Dianne grabbed Rusty's free hand and pulled him as they weave through a knot of people, children thier age stared as they pass through, more people are appearing wave by wave, the number of people are so dense that he can't see anymore where they are going.

They reached a fresh market, stands of fish and vegetables lined on either side. The crowed had thinned out, thick canvas hanged above thier head, it was thick that sunlight cant penatrate through it.

Dianne pulled Rusty out the market, they found themselves standing in front of the school, the buildings were empty, grass had grown thicker on the field the last time Rusty saw it. Sunlight had landed on the field, turning it yellow.

He-Rusty and Dianne walked pass it, Rusty's boots clanked as his heels touch the cobble stone path. They took a turn and headed for the old grocery. Rusty followed her as she climbed the stairs.

"what are we doing here?"Rusty asked peering inside the dark shop.

Dianne was about to open the door when someone shouted from the inside.

"it is better if you close this shop willy!" the voiced squeeled, it sounded convincingly like a pig's.

"Aunt Thildy" Dianne whispered ,her breath short and fast. She pulled Rusty down the stairs and into a dark pavement between two large towering stack of houses.

"aunt Thildy?"

"yes"

"she's your aunt?"

"my mother's sister"

"then why are we hiding?" he asked too loudly, Dianne hissed at him.

"she takes my money whenever she has a chance" she said her eyes on the door of the grocery. "it's your payment for my kindness,not everyone will accept you as thier niece" she imitated Thildy's piggy voice and rolled her eyes, her lips muttering soundless words of hate.

Rusty tried hard not to giggle, his face contorted into an uncomfortable smile. But deep inside him grew the amusement and pity for Dianne, how can a pale frail girl, live alone, experience all these sufferings but still survived, he stared at her face with admiration.

"cut the stares!" Dianne said without looking at him.

"s...sorry"

"it's oka...." Dianne was cutted short when the door bell chimed.

Thildy came out the door wearing a floofy yellow dress, her chin was facing the sky, her fat stubby arms wiggling at her sides. Rusty and Dianne watched her from afar as she slowly tackled the cobbled road.

Dianne and Rusty climbed the stairs again, she pushed the door slowly. The bell chimed, it echoed on the dark shop, the tiled floor was white but large particles of dust scattered on it's surface. Aisles greeted them half hidden in the darkness.

"hi willy" Dianne waved at the counter.

Willy came out, a short man wearing a red chekered shirt. There were shadows under his dcep eyes. His hair was graying, there were scars on his forehead, but Rusty knew there were more scars hidden beneath his long sleeves.

"hi....watya got me?" willy smiled at her, his voice was so raspy it could easily be a board being cut by a saw. His yellowish teeth was noticable even on the weak light of the shop.

"I've got big ones,for three boneels" she stretched her arms to show the fish.

"I'll give you the small ones for free"she nodded to the bucket on Rusty's hand. Rusty met Willy's gaze, his cold eyes hit him like spears of ice. Coldness enveloped his body his insides shivered.

Rusty swallowed and lifted the bucket up toward willy. He stared at the bucket then to Rusty then to Dianne.

"thanks" willy muttered he turned back to his counter and pulled an old icebox.

"in here" he tapped the hard plastic making a low sound. Rusty opened the ice box and poured out the fishes, he reached for Dianne's bucket and poured it out as well.

The cash register dinged and willy pulled out three silver boneels, he slided it to the counter without any noise, Dianne picked up the coins a smile was painted on her face.

"thanks willy"

"no problemo"willy knodded and return the smile, tapping the brim of his imaginary hat.

Dianne picked up the empty buckets and walked towards the door.

"bye" Rusty said lowly before turning to follow Dianne.

"bye" Willy said ,he stared at him for brief seconds before turning to pull back the old ice box.

Rusty closed the door behind him and the bell chimed.

"you know him?" Rusty asked, they were now walking on a familiar road that leads to the inn.

"yes,ive known him for years"

"then wh....what happened to willy,why is he so scary and scarry?" Dianne snorted on his question.

"Willy can be intimidating ,yes,but I dont see him as scary,he's a good guy,"

"but his voice" Rusty pointed out

"he was a soldier, the Nazis caught him,they cutted him with shards on a broken window,they even burned his leg with hot metal,he's said it was so painful he had to scream,but his screaming damaged his throat"

"he told you that?" Rusty stopped walking, horror present on his dark eyes.

"I was the only one he told"

A wave of guilt splashed on Rusty, he almost judged Willy without knowing his past. He sighed and hugged Dianne, Dianne patted his back ,

"I'm sorry,shouldn't have told you,should I?"

"n....no,you should tell me this,willy had it rough"

"he did"

Rusty let go of Dianne and picked up the buckets,he reached for her hands and laced his fingers through hers. "we need something to cool us a bit ,dont we?" . He pulled Dianne by the hand as they make thier way to the inn. He pushed the door open and the scent of different dishes reached his nose.

"good morning my good sir" the old man greeted him, his eyes stared at Rusty down into his hands, and resting on Dianne's eyes. "maam" he added quickly.

"can we have a pair of milk shakes please?" Rusty asked the old man with a smile ignoring his mocking eyebrows.

"of course sir,please get a table and wait" the old man gave a small bow and turned.

Rusty helped Dianne sit on a chair, they were sitting on the table they first met. The one beside the glass window. He wiped the non existent crumbs off the table as Dianne settles herself.

He stared at her brown eyes, she gave him a playfull smile, Rusty's heart leapt in joy. He smirked and scratched his nape, lowering his gaze.

The back door bang open, Rowlin swelled from it, his Matt hair was ruffled, dark shadows lined his eyes,

"hi Rowlin!" Rusty greeted, thankful for the welcomed disturbance.

"hmmm"Rowlin smiled at him weakly and knodded his head.

"wh...what's wrong?"

"ohhh, I got problems with Thildy,"he said simply, "nothing I can't manage" he added quickly.

"sure"

"now ,I'll leave you two alone" Rowlin took a small bow and clapped Rusty's back before dragging himself in the inn's kitchen.

"poor man," Dianne said staring at the closed door

Rusty sighed, playing with his fingertips. It saddens him that wherever he goes, there's always manipulative people.

"there you go sir"the old man arrived with a pair of milkshakes in a metal tray, he slowly placed them at the table with a few paper towels. He took a small bow and stared at the both of them, before retreating to his counter.

They chugged down the milkshake and left the inn, Rusty pulling Dianne by the hand.

"where are we going?" Dianne asked her brows furrowed.

"you'll s...see"He said, catching his breath.

They arrived in a crowded part of the town,the town square, people coming from all directions, towering building sorounded the the cement town square, plant boxes were placed at the edge of it, flowers of assorted colours adorned it.

"the square" Dianne whispered, her eyes on the people that pass them.

"yes,I saw a booth here once" he said unatentively, his head rolling ,scanning every shop his eyes can see.

"there!" Rusty pulled dianne ,a loud clang vibrated on his ear,

"wait my bucket!"

The bucket rooled on the ground, rusty picked the bucket up without letting go off her,he pulled Dianne with his hands, while the other holds the buckets.

They stopped in front of a small booth, a red curtain was draped in the entrance, he gently tugged on Dianne as he enters the booth, he stared at her smiling, she returned his smile with a more serene one.

Rusty pulled a boneel out his pocket and pushed it in the coin slot, he and Dianne smile at the small dot as it flashes every second, there was printing noise and polaroids started to pop out.

He pulled all the pictures out and flattened it on his palm. He smirked at Dianne.

"I look like an indiot on this one" he said shaking his head gently, staring ang the blurred picture on his hands, he might have moved while the picture is taken, his mouth was lopsided his eyes seemed to fall out.

"but you look cute" he pointed his fingertip on Dianne, she was beside him, but unlike him Dianne was perfectly clear. His eyes widened, he wasn't supposed to say that, was he?, Dianne giggled, pulling her hair back to her ear.

Rusty divided the polaroids, he gave three to Dianne ,and another three for himself, "thanks"she said timidly, her eyes reduced into lines,her lips streatched into a red cresent.

Rusty knodded smirking, they exited the booth hand on hand, Rusty burried the polaroids on his pocket, Dianne clutched hers holding it close to her heart.

The day went like a blurr, they roamed the town until sunset, the red sun casted light as they play tag on the beach, Rusty accompanied Dianne home when the night arrived, he waved good-bye and strolled back to his cabin.

He layed on his bed, smiling at Dianne on the Polaroid, he gave a contented growl and tucked himself on his bed as the coast of mortiana slowly sinks deeper into the night .

CHAPTER 7

"Hey rusty ,like me to help you there?" Rowlin poked his head in Rusty's door, his hair neatly brushed and tied back into a loose pony tail.

"ohh, n...no thanks,I'm almost done anyway" Rusty said shoving a pair of trousers on his bag.

"well" Rowlin smiled, his eyes sad and weak, "I'll be in my cabin if you need help" he pulled the door closed and disappeared.

Rusty turned to his bag and Shook it harshley, peeking on it's inside to make sure he packed everything.

He stared outside, the sea was playfull today, small waves crashed on the shore leaving clusters of sea foam on the sand, the sky was bright blue and barren, even the thinnest clouds can't be seen within the vicinity. The sun was set high on the sky, shining gold against blue sapphires. He poked his head out the window, warm breeze kissed him, blowing his hair as it tickled his nose and forehead. The hot sunlight landed on his face warming it up, it brought warmth to his body, his blood pulsed and circulated his viens like rivers of warm thin liquid . He sighed and smiled, staring at the line on the horizon where the sea and sky meet, where the sky and sea become one.

He pulled his head in and laid a long gaze on his cabin, the wooden bed he slept in, the blackened pots and pans that hanged on the wall of his small kitchen, the mahogany wooden table that contrasted with the dark wooden floor . He took small steps towards his bed, he slowly sit on it, and stared at his bag, he stroked the bag's surface as if it was a pet. One of his hands played with the golden ring that hanged on his neck.

The cabin's door creaked open, and Dianne came in. Her radiant smile brought the sun's light with her. Her hair was bunned loosely at the top of her head tied with a white satin ribbon. She stared at Rusty ,Rusty paid her with a weak smile, her eyes wandered around, it eventually landed on the bed, and on the large bag beside Rusty, her smile faded.

"is it today?" she asked lowly, without taking her eyes off the bag.

"ye....yeah" Rusty said ,his eyes on the floor.

Dianne sat beside him, she held his hand and gently squeezed it with both of hers. Rusty didn't look at her, her palms were soft and warm like summer. "let me take you to the station" she said almost in a whisper.

"bu...." Rusty scoofed, he never thought leaving mortania can be this hard, he loved the beach and it's sands, he loved the tall grassses that grew beside the coast, he loved the noise of the carriages when he walk town and ..... And most of all he loved her, he loved everything about her, her smooth and pale skin, her long black hair, her natural fragrance that set him off the ground, her gentle touches that send tickling sensations to his body ,her low chuckles that pinches his heart, and her downy stares that wraps him in eternal joy. But what he felt was never important, Eren came to his mind, it is best not to show Dianne any of his feelings.

"I'll.....see Rowlin first?" he asked, finally looking at her, their eyes met, his chest crumpled, he was breathing but no air enters his lungs, his insides were sore ang crying.

"of course,I'll wait here then" she said, pursing her lips into a dead smile.

Rusty pulled his hand away gently, Dianne's fingertips brushed on his skin, another wave of pain crushed his heart, as if something heavy fell on it and pounded it flat. He bit his lips and clutched his palm, his throat closed that he can't say another word. Rusty slowly open the door and left the cabin.

The outside air was warm, but he can't feel it inside his lungs, the lump on his throat slowly grew smaller, he swallowed and stared and the sun above, at least he and Dianne can share the same sun even if they're far away. He walked on the brown sand and passed on the other cabins, he reached the largest one, with the red tiled roof and thick glass windows.

He sniffed the air and knocked on the wooden door. "just a minute" Rowlin's loud voice rung on the inside "who is it?" he asked as large footsteps come nearer.

"Rusty" he said ,adressing the wooden door in front of him.

The door banged open, Rowlin smiled at him his fangs peeking through his thin dark lips.

"oh Rusty!,come in come in" he opened the door a bit too energetically and pulled Rusty in. He settled him on a three legged stool, similar to the stool he sat on when he first met Rowlin.

"so,finally leaving eh?" Rowlin pulled another stool for himself and sat in front of him.

"yes" he said, burrying his nails deep on his thigh.

"well,I'm happy I met you,Mr.Rusty" Rowlin smiled at him and placed a large hand on his shoulder. "I should thank the kind officer" he added.

"one thing Rowlin," Rusty reached for his pocket and pulled out his father's wallet. He opened the leather wallet and pulled out three trions. He handed it to Rowlin with a small smile.

"oh no Rusty,I won't accept that" Rowlin said waving his large hands in the air. "you're going home,you'll need that!"

"Yes. I'm going home so I won't need it anymore" he pushed the trions on Rowlin's chest "I just hope it can help you with Thildy"

Rowlin let out a bitter chuckle, "you're a fine lad, young rusty, a very fine lad" he said accepting the blue bills on his hands.

"you are too" Rusty said smiling at him, Rowlin let out a laugh and clapped Rusty on the back.

"one more thing Rowlin, I have a favor" he stared at the direction of his cabin.

"anything for you"Rowlin knodded.

"could you look out for Dianne?. For me" he said, his nails poking deeper on the flesh of his thigh.

"I will with all my strength" Rowlin gave another smaller knod.

"I should go now"

"goodbye and come home safe ,Rusty" he said, his voice gentle and low.

"good bye" Rusty said as he head for the door, he closed it slowly and walked away, never looking back.

He walked back to the cabin, the sand cracked under his boots, he reached his cabin's old, blackened and lined door. Rusty pushed it open and allowed himself in. Dianne was still on the bed, her hands were resting on her knees, her back slouching into a soft curve. Dianne raised her head to Rusty, she stood up and offered her hands, Rusty took it unmindedly.

"let's take a walk along the shore" she pulled him out the door by the hand.

"just a moment" he pulled back his hand and kneeled. Slowly, Rusty unlaced his boots, pulling it off his foot. He took off his brown wollen socks as well and shoved inside his boots.

Rusty then folded his trouser's leg up his calf, a white scar had formed on it, a thin white slit ran down his calf to his ankle.

He pulled up his boots by the laces on one hand, while the other reached for Dianne's, held hands they head for the shore.

Strong breezes blew on them, playing with thier hair that danced lively like the blades of the tall dry grass at the side of the coast. Dianne pulled Rusty into a run. Her face bathing in sunlight, her black hair glowed Copper like the kelps that had been washed up on the sure. There were no shadows on her face,her skin was glowing as if she was made of pure light.

Rusty's leg weakened, his heart swelled as thcy run along the shore, his surroundings melted into a dream, a dream that only have him and her,

Rusty tripped. He and dianne fell on the sand, she in top of him. He can fell her slow warm breath on his cheeks. She locked stares with him, Dianne's eyes turned bright brown her gold flecks noticable, her light body was warm against his chest.

Rusty's heart beated rapidly, his fluffy creature running around in circles, brushing every inch of his stomach. Dianne's hair fell on his cheeks, it tickled him as she push her self up. She pulled Rusty and help him dust off his chest.

He snatched her hand ,holding it gently at the wrist,"I will miss you" he looked at her eyes they were sad, he can see the dead ocean on the depths of her hazel gaze.

Dianne smiled at him sadly and removed her hands from his grip, she faced the sea and watched as a small wave approach them, the wave brought a small pink shell with it, it's had a rough textured surface. She picked it up and carressed it with her fingers. Dianne stared at him and stretched out her palms, rusty peeked at it, the shell was small enough to fit on one of her palms. She grabbed Rusty's hand and placed the shell on it.

"something to remember me"

Rusty gave the shell a long grim look, the pink colour reminds him of her pinkish cheek. He rubbed the surface of it with his thumb and smiled, his eyes still on the shell. Rusty raised his chin and faced her, he took the ring off his neck, it glinted as it danced with the breeze while hanging on the leather strap Rusty had tied it into. The gold flashed as sunlight hit it at the right angle, Rusty traced the word 'luvré' on the ring, breathing slowly. He smirked at her, a painful stab hit his chest.

"something to remember me" he reapeated.

Rusty placed the necklace on Dianne's neck, it hanged against her cream coloured dress, another breeze blew, their hair was blown in all directions, Rusty pushed her rebel strands back her ear. She stared at him ,her eyes smiling sadly, dianne clutched the ring inside her fingers pushing it deep in her chest. They exchanged smiles though Rusty was sure they both feel otherwise.

There was a high pitch whistle coming from afar followed by the roar of the steam engines and the chugging of metal wheels. Dianne reached for his hand and laced her fingers through his. She held it thight as if she never want to let go.

"cabin?" she asked him, but her stare just went through him. "cabin." she answered herself. Rusty dragged his body towards the cabin, his feet getting heavier with every breath, thier steps were large and fast, leaving dents on the sand. Shadows framed on small dunes they left behind like ranges of mountains that had been forgotten,burried on the depths of time.

They pushed the cabin's door open and walked in slowly as if approaching a sleeping beast, his heart pounded as he bended to get his bag. Dianne waited behind him, she stood still, her breathing was deep and slow. Rusty shoved the small shell down his pocket, it didn't weighed at all like it was made of the purest air. He swallowed, a lump grew on his throat. He took a deep breath and pulled the bag up his back, the weight of his stuff pulled his shoulders down, it ached as the straps burrowed deeper on his shirt.

Rusty knodded at her, he approached the door sofly and slowly turned the knob, it creaked as he slowly opened it like a whaile of banshee ready to take someone's soul. The salty air entered his lungs, it was warm as it circulated inside his chest. They stepped out the cabin, sunlight kissing thier skin. He gave the old cabin one last look before heading to the station.

Dianne remained on his tail, hiding from his sight, perhaps she was feeling too sour and bitter .he walked steadily, enduring the slowly growing pain on his shoulders. It was painful but it was numb, it was hard but it is a void, his heart was heavy but he wasn't sure if it was really.

The station's floor was misted with white steam, a number of people stood at the side of the rails, a man in a brown suit hurriedly pass them, pulling his large trunk aboard the train.

The train's head was black contrasting to the white steam it produces, Rusty reached for Dianne's hand, she grinned at him her nose crumpling, casting Rusty a playful look. Her eyes watered at the sides, her lips trembled that she looked pained, that she was using all her energy to give Rusty her best smile, a tear slid down her eye, sunshine sparkled on it like an oddly shape crystal. Rusty pulled her to his chest and wrapped his arms around her. He can feel her heart beating through his shirt, his own matched it's pace and they beated together ,their hearts danced and sung to thier own music, to thier own movement. Dianne lifted her arms and wrapped them on rusty back, her tight embrace was warm. And painful. Like the sunbeam of noon in a barren desert.

"part of me doesn't want to go,this place had been a great place for me, because mortiana has you."he whispered in her hair, warm tears formed on his own eyes ,he choked. Rusty chuckled lowly and swallowed.

"but another part of me says I need to go home,to my family,to my responsibilities " he let out a painful sigh, burrying his nose on her hair.

He cupped her cheeks at looked at her in the eye"but I promise,I will be back for you"

Dianne pushed her cheek deeper on his palms, smiling "I will wait for that time then,I promise I will wait for your return" she mirrored him at cupped his cheeks, caressing his skin with her fingertips. "I will wait, for you"

"all passengers!" a man dressed in a blue shirt poked through the window and shouted.

"all passengers, need to climb in!"

Rusty gently squeezed Dianne's hands and stared at her eyes.

"go" she whispered her lips barely moving, her words were silent like the night's air.

Rusty climbed in, the train was almost full ,passengers of diffrent statuses in one trian, there were men wearing shabby working shirts and old hats, there were others that dressed in fine silk ornated with hand embroidered pictures. Rusty poked his head out to give dianne one last look. She was standing on the dirty floor of the station, looking like the prettiest girl he ever laid his eyes on.

"where are you headed lad?"a voice asked him but he didn't took his stare off Dianne .

"Roccow"he said to the glass window, it's surfaced blurred as a mist from from his breath.

"town of Roccow . Okie dokie" he paid the voice a quick look to take his ticket and pay.

The trains engine creacked and roared the wheels started rowing, as the whistle screeched. He pushed his face deeper on the transparent surface of the window. Dianne smiled at him and waved, her hair dancing behind her back. He smiled and waved back at her.

The train started to move faster, Dianne's silhouette grew smaller, so as the station. The train roared it's wheels faster and faster, running like a bullet through air. The station became a blurr of colours as Mortiana slowly faded before Rusty's eyes.

CHAPTER 8

"So you spent your summer on that beach?,alone?" Duke asked spooning his coconut ice cream into his mouth.

"not totally alone," Rusty answered wagging his spoon on Duke's face.

"I got suspicious when your father broke down in here ,looking for you,I thought you had a fight. Again" he said ,his eyes dreamy recalling the moments when Rusty's father burst in this very shop yelling for him.

"I stole his wallet" Rusty said lowly

"you what?!" Dukes eyes widened, a small smirk appeared on his face.

"I can't survive out there without money"

"so what did they do?When you got home?"

"Lucy and George was first to greet me,then George went to tell my mother,father was oblivious ,he was shocked when I joined them on breakfast."

"he can't stay just *oblivious* forever" Duke placed his elbows on the table. His eyebrows crossing.

"no he can't. We had a fight actually" he said staring at his bowl, stirring his melted cream.

"oh,what did he do this time?" Dukes eyes stared at Rusty's, sunlight was reflected othwt, white specks scattered at the corners of his eye.

"ohh,usual. Slap and yelling and this..." He pulled down the collar of his shirt to show Duke his neck, there is a small bruise on his throat.

"ow that must hurt" Duke pointed the discolored skin.

"pssshhhhhhh" Rusty hissed and shrugged.

A very loud high pitch sound rang outside. Red and blue neon lights flashed from afar. The siren of the ambulance grew stronger, it passed the ice cream shop like a shot of wind.

"I always get scared on that siren" Rusty said.

Duke shrugged and spooned out his ice cream, his curly hair bouncing with every move, Rusty looked around the shop, it's walls were painted in cyan blue, illustrations of vines and small flowers adorned the corners, the windows were bland square, a generous amount of sunlight shone through it.

"oh here comes our sad boi" Dukes whispered, lowering his head.

"no don't look!" he stopped Rusty from turning. Rusty wondered who it was. "sad boi" he neckered.

"who?" he asked. Questionably.

The shop's glass door slid open, Rusty fought the urge to turn around, there were footsteps, it slowly thumped closer.

"oh hey Leon!" Duke greeted brightly. His eyes reduced into slits.

Rusty hurried to turn around and greet him.

"sup Leon" Leon's hair was matte and unbrushed, unusual, Rusty thought. The son of the principal was always presentable.

"hmmmmmmm" he faked a smile and knodded, walking towards the counter to get his own ice cream. Leon's shoulder grimly fell on his sides. Dark circles on his eyes were pretty-dark. Grey tinge present on his usually rosy cheek.

"what happened to him?" Rusty asked Duke, rolling his eyes, whatever the reason was , he was sure Leon deserves it. There was hatred circling inside him, he once saw Leon as *the perfect guy* ,he had a good reputation towards his peers, he had good grades ,seldomly misses any test, most of all. He was handsome. But now he's trash. He whacked Leon's head on his mind.

"Eren dumped him. I heared he asked Eren to go out with him,but she refused,she has a boyfriend from the big city" Duke whispered pushing his face closer to Rusty's.

The hatred on him, just melted and turned into pure sorry. He and Leon ,all this time, were on the same shoes. But the pain and void on his chest was nothing now, like it never existed . All he felt was warmth and joy, and Dianne.

"bad girl isn't she?" he smiled bitterly, scooping his cream to his mouth.

"SHE IS !" Duke raised his voice a bit too much, "all summer Leon tailed her ,doing everything she wants,he even runs to the bakery every-day. just to get the freshest bread we have to give it to Eren."

"did he ?"

"he did! I think Leon is madly in love"

"poor guy" Rusty clicked his tounge ,referring to both Leon and Eren's *boyfriend*.

A small beeping noise swelled from Duke's wrist underneath the thin layer of his cardigan. Duke pulled up his sleeve and took a look at his watch.

"bomb!,I need to go" Duke stood up and wiped his lip with his sleeve "the bakery?" Rusty raised his gaze towards the towering figure of Duke.

"the bakery,Ma and Da are going somewhere I need to watch the counter,catch ya later" Duke said walking to the glass door.

"bye" Rusty waved a hand to Duke's back as he ran down the cobbled street, he watched him grew smaller like a pale yellow dot on a blurr vast picture. Thick gray clouds hovering above his reddish head.

Rusty sighed and gazed above, surely gray clouds are present but patches of blue sky are visible behind it. He walked out the shop, the dusty hot air of his town slapped him, sand scratched his face like fragments of broken glass, Sweat bursted out his skin ,his hot Sweat formed beads on his shiny forehead and on the tip of his nose.

"so what are your purpose?,adornments?,a bunch of useless accessories?" he asked mockfully, sharply staring at the gray sheeps that float in the sky. He wiped his forehead with the back of his fist and walked the pavement.

Carriages occasionally passed him pulled by tall handsome horses, neighing as they gallop tiredly.

A loud tire screech traveled through the hot air, a black sleek car hastily halted in front of him, it's edges shone under the sun. George stepped out. He wasn't wearing his usual black suit but his old cacky shirt. It even seems that he had just woke up, his blue eyes looked frightened, his pupils grew so small that he seemed hyper focused. His hair was rather untidy. Strands hanged in front of his face, his loose ponytail hang rather ungraceful at his nape.

"Mr.Russel ,I....I was looking for you,please. Come with me." There was urgency on his voice. Rusty knodded and pulled himself in the car. His heart pumped harder. Have he done something wrong?, it might be really big and really offensive for his father to send George to fetch him. George stepped on the gas, the car zoomed as fast as a bullet train and tackled the inclining road. George is awfully quiet as they make thier way, his blue eyes peering through the mirror to check Rusty, Rusty gave him an encouraging knod and held his breath, his chest stiffened. The car reached the peak of the raising road, the edge of the forest is now distinguishable from afar. The beating on Rusty's chest raised three numbers, blood rushed to his face as his cheeks and ear heatened. He noticed that he was clutching his fist rather too tight, the viens on his arm form large bumpy lines, his knuckles whitened, his fingertips turned papery. The car entered the forest, leaves and twigs cracked under the tires, small branches brushed the car's roof ,grass blades tickled it's underside, like small green limbs reaching out for them from the depths of he'll.

Sunlight became more and more scarce, the thick canopy above their heads refused to let the sunlight hit the forest floor. A few couples of sunbeams manage to swell through the thick layers of leaves, like beacons of gold in the middle of pale darkness. George coughed, he avoided to stare at the mirror but Rusty saw something was wrong with his eyes. They were..... restless.

"George?.....George. What's the matter?"

"I...I'll tell you at the Manor sir."George stirred the wheel and avoided Rusty's eyes then.

The forest begun to thin out, tall grass replaced the thick trees, the car glided through the yellow field, sunshine poured and rained on them, Rusty had to blink to adapt to such brightness. The Manor appeared in front of them, Lucy was at the front door waiting for them.

"ohh Rusty!," she shouted as Rusty hopped off the car, she trapped him on her arms as she begun to sub, large beads of tears ran down her wrinkly cheek, her nose was red, her eyes swollen and half opened. George rubbed Lucy's back like a child comforting his mother.

"wha...what happened ?,tell me." he raised his head to meet Lucy's, Lucy sobbed louder, her voice cracked as she drowns on her own tears.

"it's....it's....your parents " she said between sobs. She burried her nose on her embroidered flowery hanky and blew her nose on it.

"Mr.and Mrs. Luvré had an accident sir" George answered on Lucy's behalf, when he noticed that Lucy was too weak to tell Rusty.

"wha....what?" His chest crumpled, that can't be true!, his mother is perfectly safe.

"the...they had an accident.....accident in....the factory " Lucy regained herself, tears still flow freely on her eyes.

CHAPTER 9

Rusty was staring at his reflection,his tired and red eyes stared back at him. His lips were red but painfully grim.

What have he done to deserve this?

He put on his necktie,but he cant make it sit perfectly on his chest . He blew off a long and slow breath,squeezing the tie he cant manage to put on.

There was a soft knock on the door, it sounded so distant as if Rusty was on the edge of the universe. Like he was standing on the void of space , his mind scattered as as he slowly melts into the void, becoming one with the void himself.

The door slowly creaked open ,producing agonizing sounds ,is it really? or is it just him?

Lucy entered through the door. She was dressed in a satin back blouse, her long skirt barely touched the floor as she glided towards Rusty. Her black satin clothing reminded Rusty of the night his father left him beside the road.

"are you ready ,Rusty dear?"Lucy asked,her voice was so cracky her throat must have ripped. She pulled out a lacy hanky and dabbed the corners of her eyes. if red isnt a real colour, Rusty wouldnt know how to describe it.

Rusty sighed. He knows that it wont do anything, but it is all he could do at the moment."almost".

Lucy smiled at him weakly. Very weakly. She gently tugged the tie on Rusty's neck and knotted it into perfect shape.

"we need to go" Lucy stared at his reflection. She and Rusty met eyes ,he can see the void in them. And the darkness through her eyes .He can see pure sadness. He can see the depth of the sea, both dark and cold.

Rusty knodded ,addressing Lucy through the mirror. Lucy patted his back gently before leaving . Sniffing siently as she opens the door. Her slow steps rung on Rusty's ear. Now that it turned so quiet ,he can hear his own heart beat. The manor had never been noisy and chaotic, but today it was more silent than usual. Worse than just mere silence.

Rain drops trickled over the town.The icy raindrops made small noises as they hit suface, like screams of little humans. Weak gust of wind played with the airborne drops from time to time. The drops hit painfully on Rusty's skin.

Few people attended the funeral. The fewest Rusty had ever seen. Not that he attended that much funerals. Rusty knew them as thier bussiness partners and the local officials.

Pain pounded on Rusty's chest. In his mind he was screaming . He cant count how many times he did it. It wasnt supposed to be like this. It was not at all.His mother was a great woman ,she cared for him. Tears appeared on the corner of his eyes. It was warm compared to the rain. She loved him,his mother was one of the gentlest beings he knew. Rusty remembered her downy stares, he will miss those.

And his father. It is true that he and his father don't get along very well, but as his child, Rusty loved him. Tears fell down from his eyes, rolling down his cheek. He scoof a very painful scoof ,it was so painful he can taste the air growing bitter. He was alone, and now he IS alone. Rusty:the last Luvré .

Someone placed a hand on his shoulder, he would have flinched but he didn't. "I wish I have the words to make you feel better, but I know I don't. " William's voice echoed in his ear. He faced him smiling weakly. William tightened his grip on Rusty's shoulder. "I'm here for you". Rusty stared into his eyes and knodded, he trusted William the first time thier eyes met on the hospital, he don't know why, but he is glad he did.

They- Rusty and William faced the pile of fresh unearthed dirt. A small plaque made from granite was placed above it. Ingraved in gold letters says "Edward and Sarah Luvré ".

Just beside it lies another grave having the same shiny granite plaque and the same golden letters but says "Benjamine Luvré".

"Luvré? ", William noticed the neighbouring grave.

"Yes"

"Is he your uncle or something?"

"He's my brother. I call him ben, he passed away when I was twelve. Two years ago. "

"H.. How? " William asked, not breaking his stare on the plaque.

"His car hit a line post on his way to school to pick me up" Rusty said ,looking on the plaque too.

"I... I'm sorry, that was insensitive of me to ask", William said finally looking at Rusty.

"You're 18 aren't you?, if ben was alive he'd be your age. You and George" Rusty stared at the blonde boy walking towards them.

"Mr. Russle" George started but Rusty cutted him short.

"Rusty",he stared at William as well, William knodded knowing-ly.

"By the way, George this is William, you might have seen him on the factory, and William this is George" Rusty introduced each other, they-William and George exchange small knods.

"R... rusty, Lucy is looking for you" Rusty knodded at George and bid goodbye to William. He was about to leave when the mayor in his red tail coat called him. Shouting his last name, grinning. His white sparkly teeth, shone even under the Grey sky.

"Quite disrespectful I would say" George whispered but the wind brought his voice to Rusty's ear.

"Is he?" William asked sarcastically, eyeing the mayor sharply.

The mayor seemed not to hear them over the confidence he's wearing. He flashed his high chest at the three of them. His belly was fuller the last night's moon. The buttons of his tailcoat might snap off any moment.

"I won't waste your time Mr. Luvré" he smiled greedily. "A factory isn't easy to run, I am here. Not just as mayor, but a concerned individual, I am offering my kindness, Mr. Luvré. Name your price I will buy the factory."

Rusty's ear heatened ,he frowned at the mayor's piggy face.

"I dont think this is the perfect time for that Mr. Mayor" William said politely. He placed his hand on Rusty's shoulder, pulling him closer.

"On the contrary, I think this is the perfect time" Rusty said, a grin stretched across the mayor's face.

"It is my boy, now. Name your price"

"Iwon't name any price. Mr. Mayor" he said flatly, dully staring at the mayor like he was nothing but a curtain of mist. "I will keep the factory" the grin vanished from the mayor's mouth, his jaw fell ajar making him look like a bewildered boar.

"I mere child like you can't run a factory!,you will face proble ms.hard problems!" the mayor exclaimed, clearly heated.

"If the child believes in hisself, sir. Who are we to doubt him? Best we do is support him" William said not losing his politeness.

"Are you dumb, young man? That is a child! " the mayor said ,his eyes jumping between Rusty and William.

"The child has a name. Sir. And no. I am not dumb, are you?" William asked at the falttest tone Rusty has ever heard, he made a self note not to challenge him in any game of sarcasm.

The mayor was taken aback, his lips shivered, his mustache trembled. But no words came from him. He cleared his throat and seemed to redeem himself.

"A child can't run a factory, soon he will face problems ,hard massive problems!, how can a child handle those?! " the mayor pointed Rusty in full disbelief.

"George here and I will make sure he won't face those" William said stiffly, George knodded with stern eyes, Rusty was grateful for William. And George. As believable as it sound, Rusty knew that one-day, Maybe sooner maybe later,he will have to face conflicts regarding the factory.

"now Mr. Luvré, aren't you in a hurry? ,off you go now. " William pushed Rusty gently away from the mayor and towards thier black family car.

"I could've defended myself " he said as he pulls the car's door open.

"I know" William replied quietly "go now, I bet my brother is waiting for me" he tapped the brim of his hat and bowed, before running to the other end of the road.

Rusty allowed himself in, Lucy was up front beside George. She turned to him and gave him a weak painful smile, Rusty knew she meant to reassure him, it's not working. She hurriedly turned back to secretly wipe her eye with her lacey hankee, Rusty saw it through the reflection on the car window.

The car engine started, it roared alive rather too loudly, the car Shook a bit too much. The car stirred through the damp road, yes it was damp but Rusty find it too wet. What is wrong with him. Everything.

The trickling rain haven't seized since they arrived home. Is it still home afterall?, Rusty honestly don't know. He was lying at the yellow field, trying to drown his sadness on the weak weeping rain drops. Mud stucked on his nape as he sinks deeper in the mushy ground everytime he moves and sighs. The sky had gone completely dark, thick layers of chiffon clouds blanketed Rusty's world, his skin had goosebumps, he knew it was cold, but he can't feel it anymore, he was cold himself. He pulled himself up, every inch of his body ached, even when he breathes a small popping pain pierces his chest, if this is not the most painful pain, pain is not real at all. He dragged his feet, the soles of his boots glided on the yellowish grass blades of the field. Left right left right, he narated his steps ,I know how to walk,thank you. He straightened his body, it cramped like his spine was stretched inside of him, he might have slouched for so long. Rusty glanced at the Manor, it was a beacon of beauty, tall pines bordered the garden, gardenia flowers shines pearly white even in the distance, those were his mother's favorite. It was beautiful indeed. It was just a shame, he can't seem to appreciate it, not this time.

Rusty pushed the manor's front door open, it swayed elegantly, noise less, as normal, at least something remained the same. He was greeted by the parlor, a huge spacious room, where they normally held thier parties, the room was dark, no one bothered to turn on the lights, except for a small candle glass, it's warm honey light was so weak it only lit the table it was placed on. Rusty can make out a pair of silhouettes sitting at the parlor's chair set.

"Lucy, Rusty's here",George said.

Rusty walked nearer. Lucy was sobbing, her old wrinkled hands covering her face, George was beside her, rubbing her back and shoulders.

"Rusty dear, would you like me to cook something for you? " Lucy asked sniffing uncontrolably.

"No thanks Lucy, you can rest" Rusty stooped in front of her and kissed her. It is true, it is painful. But he can't be like this forever, Lucy had been part of thier lives, as well as George, he needs to be strong for them, they're the only family he has left. He clenched his body, as if all his loose flesh slapped back to thier places. He stood up and stared at George.

"We'll be leaving early tommorow"

"To where? "

"The factory" he turned and started for the stairs.

"Yes Rusty"

Rusty climbed the stairs, it was creaky, his body was all sore and tired like he had ran a thousand miles non stop. He might need a rest. He entered his room, Rusty never bothered to turn on the light, creeping in the darkness he washed his skin and dried it, pulling on his clothes and fall on his bed. He breathe very slowly. Lying in his chest, he stared into nothingness. Tears swelled from his eyes, he cried all his pain ,not out but it calmed him, his breath became shallow as he drifted into sleep.

"You dont look great" George said as he drives.

Rusty knew, but looked at hisself still. Through the window's reflection he can see his face, dark circles edged his eyes. His eyes. They were droopy, sleepy. Tired. "Would they notice? " he asked although he knew the answer.

"Absolutely" George replied.

The car stirred into a pebbly parkway. The factory's parkway. Rusty stared at the big white structure nearby, an illustration of a barn in a blue background was painted on the factory's entrance.

"This is it, you can go home now George, Lucy is alone"

"She strictly told me to look after you today, said she'll be fine"

"Fine"Rusty said as he walk towards the factory. George tailed behind him.

Pebbles cracked on his boots as he steps, he might take it out, it's quite the effort to keep balance in these. Machines buzzes and bottles clank as he entered the factory. He sighted William on the butter wrapping aisle, conversing with one of the lead wrappers.

"Oi", George said as they approach him.

"Good Morrow George, Rusty why are you here?, you look quite pale, are you okay?" William asked studying Rusty's features.

"I'm fine"Rusty said sternly. "Have you seen Bella?, I might have something to ask her"

"Dolphy here can help us" William addressed the woman he was conversing with, "could you fetch Bella for us?, we will wait for her at Mr. Luvré's office" Dolphy knodded smiling.

"She's at the stocks with Robert, thank you Dolphy" William said courtly.

Dolphy immediately set off, her gray blouse shakes as she bounces on her heels as she steps. William smiled at Rusty.

"After you Mr. Luvré" Rusty led the way and tackled the metal stairs to the third floor, the stairs was winding to save space, it is the only stair that is. That particular stairs led to his father's office. The office was large, thick walls of glass enabled them to oversee the factory without actually leaving the office.

"Take a seat Mr. Luvré, Bella might be here any moment now", William pulled the whelled workchair off Rusty's father's desk and invited Rusty to seat.

"Sit with me George" William patted a seat beside him on a maroon velvet sofa, George undone his lowest button of his suit and sat beside William. It was funny how they contrast with each other, George having blonde hair and black suit while William has dark hair and pristinely white one.

There was a soft knock and Bella appeared, she was the secretary of Rusty's late father, Bella made her way to Rusty her purple pencil skirt complemented her crimson nails.

"You called me sir Russle? "

"Yes Bella, I... I want you to call everyone, the heads of each station and our partners, I have.... Have an anouncement to make"

"Yes sir Russle" Bella hurriedly left the room ,the heels of her shoes made funny noises as she did so.

Rusty knodded at William, giving him a let's go look. "George, you should attend too" he said when George hesitated to get up.

" but Rusty, I don't have business being there"

"Yes of course you have, I want you to assess William, be his secretary, you want to look after me don't you?"

"Yes Rusty"

"Call him sir, when we're in the office, let's be professional " William patted George's chest and whispered.

"Yes,Mr. Luvré sir" George restated ,William gave him an approving look.

The three of them caravaned into the conference room, just below Rusty's office. William held the door for Rusty, he knodded courtly before pushing himself in.

Everyone was already there, his business partners, he recognized Robert amongst them, and his high ranking staff. Rusty stared at everyone with power and sat on the seat Bella reserved for him.

"Thank you for coming everyone"

"Of course sir, " and elderly man replied, his face was droppy, his hair white on the edges.

"My... My parents had passed on a car accident just a couple of days ago, and they left the company hanging with no one to take care, so here I am, proposing myself as a Luvré to run the factory", Rusty prepared himself ,He knew someone is against it.

"But sir, can you handle the factory and the paper works?", he was right, the elderly man questioned him.

"I was trained by my father, I'm confident I can manage" he faked his confidence.

"This is foolishness, why would we trust our money on the hands of a young boy? " a woman in her middle age babbled.

"Fourteen it is, and it's not that young, I can think as sane as you do" he replied, the woman looked fuzzled.

"If you have too many question about Mr. Luvré's ability to run the company, maybe you would like the mayor to take over" William said politely, his voice was calm and firm.

"What do you mean? " the staff chorused.

"The mayor had offered money, if Mr. Luvré will sell the company, he could return everyone's shares, but he did not" William said.

"This company is my parent's legacy, I want to take care of it, anyone has any More questions? " he asked the air, though he hope there is none.

Everyone stayed quiet, Rusty hid a smile.

"Very well, that's all for my announcement " he said.

Everyone left thier seats and left, a few of them Shook Rusty's hand, wished him good. One of them is Robert Canoir.

"Congratulations on your first meeting Mr. Luvré, if you need help you can count on me and my brother" Robert said, smiling at Rusty.

CHAPTER 10

"Mr. Luvré!, Sir William is waiting in the car, we need to go" George said to Rusty.

Rusty had arranged a meeting with potential client, an owner of a large and famous ice cream brand on the big city. This will be his first client . If he can close the deal.

"Let's go " he replied, George stormed out the office in a hurry, his shoulder length blonde hair was significantly more tamed and managed. Rusty followed him, uneasiness building inside him.

"Okay, Mr. Darren is a busy man, he hates wasting time, it is best we don't keep him waiting, the meeting is on three, driving to the big city can take almost an hour, if we leave now we'll be there by 2:30" William said without pause as soon as Rusty settled on a seat.

"Hello to you too William" he replied. Strange. William was always the one to greet first.

"Hi" he smiled sheepishly.

"Tensed, ain't you sir? " George asked. Staring at William through the mirror, as he starts the engine.

"Oh darling, isn't that too obvious? " William said, admitting it. " Robert was supposed to acompany Rusty"

"What's happened?" George asked stirring the wheel as the car slowly advances out the factory's driveway.

"He had a meeting with another client, a grocery owner in Keinsevee" he said looking at George's back, before turning to Rusty. " I trust he told you that? "

"Yes he did, he gave me a call earlier"

"Good!, he can be a bit.....forgetful sometimes, tho I have a feeling he's faking it"

"Is that so? " George asked.

"Yes!, he intentionally forgets I'm his brother sometimes ",William said frustratedly.

Rusty choked a laugh, he tried to contain it but the more he hide it the larger his smirk become. George burst out in laughter. Rusty and William joined in.

The three of them babbled as thier car glided on the outskirts of Rocco. Tall unkept trees bordered the forest not so far away, the road turned rough and unflat. They passed on small cottages with pens for livestock from time to time, it greatly differs from Rocco's central where roads are stone and homes are more cramped.

Rusty felt his bottom getting numd, he must be sitting for more than half an hour. Soon large, tall buildings begun to grow on the horizon, the big city is getting closer.

" about forty minutes , we arrived earlier than my calculations. " William said, looking at his watch. " great job George"

" of course, darling" George said proudly, he stepped on the gas, and the car moved faster, the car hit smooth land and the highway begun, more and more cars appeared in sight, George slowed down when too many cars had flocked beside them as they drive closer to the heart of the city.

George pulled a stop on a parkway near a cafe, Rusty opened the car door and slided out. He immediately breathed the smoky hot air of the city, a gust blew on them ,his hair swayed, dust entered his eyes.

" well, not that inviting" he said rubbing his eyes.

"Yep, but you'll get used to it" William said beside him.

"Why would Mr. Darren meet a supplier in a cafe? Mr. Darren, someone who for sure has a cozy office" George murmured, inspecting the cafe in front of them.

"It's easier to turn down a deal here, I reckon we all know Mr. Darren sees us as a puny company, he doesn't want to make a fuss out of this.... Partnership" William answered George, staring at both Rusty and him dully.

"Let's prove him we're better than he thinks" Rusty said with all his heart, except for the very minuscule part that agrees with Mr. Darren.

"Let's wait inside, being diligent might impress him. Hopefully" William pushed the cafe's door open, a small bell chimed, announcing thier presence.

"Hello there sirs, can I get you something? " a young man approached them from the counter. He was wearing a brown apron over a cream long sleeved shirt.

"Let me show you your seats" he said and motioned them to follow him, he showed them a table larger than the others, it's has six chairs while the others only has a pair. They seated themselves on one side of table.

"First time here?, would you like me to show you our menu? , we also have pastries" the man offered.

"Could we wait for someone first? " William asked politely.

"Of course sir" the man responded smiling.

"Thank you. We'll call you when we're ready"

The man took a bow and retreated to his counter, where another man was stationed wearing the same apron and shirt. They wiped the mugs and arranged thier coffee jars while waiting for costumers.

"It's almost 3,he might be here any moment" William said tapping his fingertips on the wooden table.

Not a lot of moments later Mr. Darren arrived,his secretary tailing at his back. The cafe door struck open, the bell chimed agressively. He could have opened it gentler, Rusty thought. The three of them snapped into a stiff stand.

"Ahhhh Mr. Luvré!, thought I'm earlier than you" Mr. Darren reached out a hand to William smiling widely, it is obvious he is faking it. His eyes were akward.

"I'm sorry sir, but I am not Mr. Luvré" William said but shook his hand anyway.

" oh! my bad, Mr. Luvré" Mr. Darren reached for George.

"No sir, I'm the secretary " George Shook hands with Mr. Darren as well.

Mr. Darren's face glumped off, he stared at Rusty with full disbelief.

"Mr. Luvré? "

"Yes sir" Rusty reached out a hand towards Mr. Darren. He stared at it for long seconds, his eyes jumped between Rusty and his stucked out hand. He clapped hands with Rusty's but didn't shook it.

"Have a seat please sir " Rusty offered the other of the side of the table, Mr. Darren's party sat at the opposite side.

"Coffee sir" He said and called the cafe waiter.

He walked over to them smiling "what would you like today sirs and miss? "

"We'll have black coffee "said Mr. Darren on the behalf of his secretary.

"Three cappuccinos please" Rusty said

" cakes? " he asked everyone

" we're fine " Mr. Darren answered dully.

"That's all thank you" Rusty finished.

The waiter knodded and walked back to the counter.

"Mr. Darren you have a v-" Rusty started

"Are you pulling pranks?, i'll be honest I hate playing the fool"
Mr. Darren said.

"Of course not sir"

" you are really Mr. Luvré? "

" yes"

Mr. Darren pinched the bridge of his nose, his eyes close as he
widraws air. He stared at Rusty like he's a clown. "Okay Mr. Luvré,
what do you got? "

Rusty stared at George. George handed Rusty a folder of thier
files. " this is our sales for the past months sir, and a copy of some
satisfactory messages from our past clients"

Mr. Darren accepted the papers and paid short glances at it as
he rapidly switch from page to page. " I see, Mr. Uhhhh... "

"Russle sir, Russle Luvré "

"Here's your coffee sir, thank you for waiting" the waiter arrived
with thier order, he gently transfered the cups of coffee unto
the table, cutting the conversation. He took a small bow and left
quietly.

" Mr. Russle, I run a big brand, people expects me to only serve
them the best quality I could offer"

" I fully understand that sir, our company produces the highest
quality dairy all across Rocco"

Mr. Darren smiled flatly, is that even a smile?, Rusty thought no.
"Of course"

" you are a child Mr. Russle, why are you running your company? Aren't your parents supposed to do the marketing ?" Rusty knew he would ask about his parents.

"They're supposed to do it if they're still alive sir. My parents passed on a month ago" he said it all in one single breath.

"I'm sorry Mr. Russle" said Mr. Darren his words were covered in insincere sweetness.

" that's all right Mr. Darren" he smiled at him, a forced smile it is.

Mr. Darren took a sip of his coffee, so as his secretary. "That's all I need to know, I'll call you later this evening Mr. Russle, for my decision"

" I'll be sure to answer sir"

" you better be" Mr. Darren said chuckling.

He raised from his seat and knodded at everyone. Turning to leave.

"Walk him back to his car, I'll pay for these" William whispered, his eyes on Mr. Darren's back.

Rusty knodded and followed Mr. Darren. " could I walk you back sir?"

" you may" Mr. Darren opened the door and walked out the cafe rather fast. Rusty assumed that his car was the gray, expensive looking one at the corner. Mr. Darren was walking that way. And Rusty was right, he stopped at the very front of it. The car's window sank down as a girl poked her head out. " took you long enough" she said ,eyes sharp.

" I'm sorry dear" Mr. Darren said, pulling the driver's door open.

Rusty and the girl met eyes, he gave her a shy smile and a small bow. The girl stared at him sharply but returned his smile with an evil looking grin. The car's engine started ,it speared through the air, feeding Rusty dark fumes.

"Aren't meetings supposed to last longer? " Rusty asked no one in particular as their car drove back to Rocco. He rests his forehead against the glass, glancing outside the mix of colours that pass his eyes.

"They're supposed to be" William said massaging his temples.

"Allright you too? " George asked. "You look fried"

" I'm not fried! , I'm burnt! He rejected me the first time he laid me a glance! "Rusty exclaimed I'm frustration.

"Calm down, maybe Mr. Darren is just like that to everyone" George said, keeping his eyes on the road for they are about to take a narrow turn.

" we can hope, but I'm not optimistic if I'mma be honest" William said, eyes closed, his fingers was still pressed on his temples.

"We'll know this evening " Rusty said and pushed his back deeper on the car seat, sinking into a more comfortable slump.

Rusty might have slept on the way for when he opened his eyes Geroge was pulling the car towards the Manor garage.

"I might have dozed-off" he said rubbing his eyes, " where's william? "

" I dropped him on the factory" George said, taking off his seat belt. He gently hopped out the car and walked around it. He tugged on the car's back door and opened it for Rusty.

"Thanks" Rusty thanked him, hopping off the car himself.

George gave him a smile and put an arm an his shoulder. They walked towards the Manor door. George pushed it and waited for Rusty to get inside before closing it again.

" you're home " Lucy smiled at them, examining thier faces. " I'm preparing dinner, you can rest for now " she smiled, her mild cherry perfume stained the manor' s air.

Rusty ascended the stairs up to the second floor, he stopped in front the first door. It was made of red wood heavely carved with flora and long plumed fowls. Behind the door was a room. His parent's room. He sniffed breifly and turned the door knub, it swayed with minimal noise. The room was full of tall shelves, a desk was placed afront the window, inches tall of papers stacked above it, the dimming sunlight poured over the yellowish pile of paper, he caressed the topmost paper. It has his father's signature on it, it was an order form of new machineries.He genty put it back, so gentle ,so demure that the paper slid perfectly back to it's place.

"Rusty dear?! " Lucy haistely opened the door " I looked for for you in the other room but you weren't there "

" uh yeah, I.... I was just looking at the room"

Lucy observed the room as well but Shook her remenisence off. " you have a call"

" already?!" He asked shock, he left Lucy behind and hurriedly stepped down the stares, if he could just jump it down he would have.

"It's Mr. Darren" George mouthed as Rusty approached. " yes Mr. Darren, here is Mr. Luvré" George handed him the phone and whispered "good luck"

Rusty gulped and took the phone, he placed it's earpiece to the side of his face. " good evening Mr. Darren"

"Good evening Mr. Luvré, but I have to ask your forgiveness"

Rusty gulped again, squeezing the phone.

"I have reviewed your sales Mr. Luvré, it is impressive I'll be honest, and your cream do taste great, tried it myself"

" thank you sir, yes our cream is high quality, it's made with the most advanced machine-"

" but I have to refuse the contract, Rocco is too far from the big city and your cream taste different than the cream we use for our product, I hope you understand Mr. Luvré " Said Mr. Darren, but Rusty thought he heared chuckles between his lines.

"I do understand sir but pl-" Rusty answered but the line cut off. Rusty's guts twisted and turned in an awful way, his eyes heatened ,his throat swelled up.

"What's he say? " George asked, his eyes hopeful.

"He declined us" he said but no voice came from him, George read his lips and glumped. He moved closer and rubbed Rusty's hair.

"That's okay, we'll find another client, I'll work harder to find one" George lowly said. Rusty didn't respond he remained his head bowed and balled his fist. "That's okay" George repeated louder.

" let's fill your tumtum to warm your mood up, dinner's ready" George maneuvered him and seated him on the table. George patted his back and asked "You want mash potatoes? " he filled Rusty's plate with steak and a spoonful of mashed potatoes. He placed it in front of Rusty, George handed him the utensils smiling slightly with a " that's allright" look.

"I'm fine" Rusty sniffed and returned his smile. George's smile grew bigger, he turned to Lucy with a "see? I'm that great" look. Lucy chuckled cutting her steak.

Rusty was at his room preparing to sleep, his bed was ready only waiting for him, the pair of pillows looked inviting, the freshly pressed blanket did as well. But, there was a soft knock at the door, the knob turned slowly, the door opened.

"Rusty, there's a call for you" Gorge said without letting himself in completely. He and Rusty hurried downstairs, the phone laid on the parlor desk, Rusty picked it up.

"Hello, this is Mr. Luvré"

"Finally! I wanted to ask forgiveness about my father's way of treating you" said a girl's voice from the other line

"Uhh... Who's this?, if I may ask"

" oh, yes.I'm sorry, I'm Sherley. Sherley Darren, daughter of Lune Darren, the same Mr. Darren that called you earlier " she said boredly, as if she, even herself was tired of her identity.

"Nice to meet you Ms. Sherley, and don't worry I understand your father"Rusty said politely, faking a smile as if Sherley on the other line could see it.

"No, I'll convince my father to get you as our supplier " she said hurriedly " and if I did"

Rusty slightly thought it wasn't for free, and he was right, sometimes he wonder why not be a furtune teller instead ,after all his guesses are most of the time but not always true. "And if you did? " he repeated.

"If I did, you'll agree to be my boyfriend " she said in a tone of pure confidence.

"I.... I.. " a large smile crept on Rusty's face, different from his awful fake smile, it is a smile of vile purpose.

"Yes you. You what? " she asked impatiently.

"I'll be your boyfriend " he said, the grin still plastered on his face. "If you could change his mind"

"Just wait and see" she cackled and hung up.

Rusty let go of the phone and stared at George. George stared back at him, his eyes puzzled, his mouth hanged ajar.

"You did not" George said in a voice full of disbelief.

"I did" he replied knodding, " turns out we still have a chance "

George sighed at him shaking his head very slowly. He moved closer and placed a hand on his shoulder, grasping it squeezing it tight.

CHAPTER 11

It had been ten years since Rusty recieved a phone call from Sherley. Sherly is the daughter of Mr. Darren- a client that turned down thier partnership, luckily Sherley was able to revoke her father's mind and in return Rusty should agree to be his boyfriend.

Rusty was waiting for sherley in a mall on the big city, since they became "officially on" Rusty had been busy traveling to and fro the big city. He sighed. Plucking the invisible hairs on his collar. The mall was busy, people passed him like a swarm of different colours, it strucks him to see how different big city was from Rocco, in the past ten years the city trend on clothing changed rapidly like a train full of steam. Whilst Rocco remained on thier plain white shirts and fluid dresses.

"Honey ,dear! There you are! " he heard Sherley from afar, he turned towards her mastering a wide half-fake half-almost real smile. Sherley waved at him and ran his way, her short tight skirt was so stiff it seemed unnatural .

"Hi" he greeted her.

"Wanna watch a movie today?" She asked enthusiastly.

"Okay, but I need to go back early, the factory is kinda busy"

"Do I care? " she asked eyeing him neither too sharp not dull either, but it was nothing sweet and gentle.

"I.... I" he stuttered, not knowing what to answer.

" you are going to stay with me the whole day" she said and turn back then walked in a pace that seemed too unnatural, it's as if she wanted to leave but she also slows down as if she wanted him to follow, but when he does she raises it again.

"Okay fine, fine I'll stay with you" he said tired of her game, he closed his eyes to keep it from rolling.

"You must" she said finally looking back at him, "or my father would cancel this month's order" she pulled Rusty in a movie theater inside the mall, he paid for thier entry as she wiggles ahead looking for seats.

"Want popcorn sir? " the ticket handler offered. The boy looked on his early 20's but is younger than Rusty.

"No thank you, she doesn't like popcorns" he looked at her with heavy eyes.

"I see" the boy quietly said ,eyeing at Sherly as well.

"I'll get drinks instead" he said faking his energy.

"Of course sir, whatya want? "

"Soda, two of your largest cup" he said smiling.

The boy handed him two waxed carton cups full of thier fizzy soda. Rusty slided a gold shelly, the boy picked it up and slided back four bronze suds.

"Thank you" Rusty smiled.

"Thank you" the boy repeated, bowing.

He grasped the cups on his hand and followed Sherley. She managed to get seats at the front row, but he's sure those seats were occupied earlier.

"finally, took you long enough" she muttered her eyes on the big screen.

" sorry,but I got these" he handed her the cups .

"Oh! Goodie!" She grabbed the cups from Rusty rather harshley,Rusty looked at her unimpressed but not surprised. Sherley haistely sipped on one cup not taking her eyes off the screen.

"There you go"he handed him back the cup. She smiled at him cutely. She not-not at all.

"Why thank you" he smiled at her weakly, a really small smile.

"Of course honey dear" she stared at him and moved closer, pressing a smootch on his cheek.

Rusty chuckled uncomfortably and wiped his sticky cheek with his sleeve. He Shook the cup, it was half empty. Was it half empty? Or was it half full?, why does it matter really?.

He slumped on the chair deeper, but didn't got comfortable, They were watching a high energy action movie, tho black and white in colour the flash of firing bullets from the actor's gun dazzled Rusty, every now and then Sherley would squeeze his arm. He sighed really lowly surrendering.

It was a pretty boring movie, Rusty never liked the intense shouts and barbaric personality of the characters. His bottom felt numb, he pounded it with his fist to somehow bring feeling back into it.

"Great movie isn't it?, I like how Tony jumped on the bridge right before the ending" she screamed on his ear.

Rusty pulled his head away and said " yes! A very great movie indeed " though he don't know who is Tony.

"We should go shopping" Sherley pulled him into a stall within the mall that is mainly dedicated to the latest fashion trends of the most famoust brands. Rusty allowed her to pull the whole life out of him. He stiffly smiled behind her, greeting everyone back on her behalf. He avoided to look at the mirrors which covered the shops walls, he know he looked like and idiot with his smile but he don't want to see any more proofs.

Sherley slithered and hopped every shop her eyes can reach, Rusty tailing at her back holding the hundred bags from her earlier purchases. He saw a clock placed on a wall and tried to read the time. It was already 4' in the afternoon, they were shopping for six hours already.

"Awwww already?! " she screamed in frustration when she too looked at the clock.

"We can continue shopping another time" Rusty gently said, shaking the bags on his hands, his fingers and wrist we're burning red because of the cheap ropes from the bags that scratched him, not to mention the combined weight of at least two dozen clothes.

" ehhhhh" she grunted, " I won't buy from this mall again at the moment, thier clothes isn't good looking at all.

"Of course" he said knobbing. SMILING. then eyeing the bags that clung on his wrist and fingers.

"Drive me home" she said, massaging the back of her neck.

" but what about your driver? "

"Ehh forget about him" she flicked her hand in the air as if chasing a large fly away.

"I should tell him at least"

" I said FOR-GET-HIM" she a said wide eyed.

Rusty smiled at her and knodded .again. It was all he could do anyway. " let's go"

"mmmkay" Sherley smiled sheepishly and clung on his arm.

Sherley hops too much when walking, bouncing on the balls of her feet even though she wears heels. Rusty needed to match her slow up-and -down pace. He wish he need not.

Rusty threw the paper bags at the back of his car when they reached the parking lobby. Those bags was annoying him. He opened the back door for Sherley to scoot in.

"Excuse me?! " she asked scandalized before pulling the rear door open and pulled it close shut creating a really loud snap.

"What's that for? " he asked trying to keep himself.

"I'm your girlfriend Russle!, I will be your spouse someday, was that the way to treat your spouse?

"Look, I...im sorry... Okay" he said taking the driver's seat. " forgive me" he stared at her.

Sherley smiled at him and threw her arms open wide. She pulled Rusty into a hug, "okay" she said and kissed Rusty on the cheek. Rusty as well wrapped his arms around her back and rubbed it in circles.

He drove her home, listening to her endless cackle on the way. He waved at her good-bye, and drove his own way home. Sunset accompanied him, throwing him tangerine rays at his window as the wind raced with him. Dust floated behind him leaving a ghostly cloud in the middle of a growing night.

"Hey I'm home! " He greeted no one at particular .

"Ohhh eyy Rusty" George waved at him, he was on the phone ,the smooth surface of it reflected the dimming light outside the window. " he's here" he said to the phone

"Who's that? " Rusty mouthed, George understood him and answered "it's William"

"Tell him I'll work tomorrow "

George knodded " yes!, Our Little Rusty will be there tommorow, and that is certain" George knodded as he listens to William on the other line. " of course, good night to you as well" George sat down the phone and turned to Rusty. He scanned him up and down, he frowned, looking at Rusty's hand.

"Are they alright?" He pulled Rusty's hand towards him, tracing the small red scratches with his eyes.

"They're fine, but my belly isn't"

George chuckled and placed a hand on his shoulder,they made their way to the kitchen through the vacant dining room which had been lighted with small bulbs of incandescent light.

"Oh it's almost time for dinner" Lucy smiled at both of them. Carrying the plate to the table, she placed the sparkling China down the redwood table and threw them inviting glances. Rusty and George more than willingly took thier seats and settled themselves. Lucy served them dinner ladling soup, and handing them the plate of smoked meat.

"Had fun today? " She asked eyeing both of them.

" yes, William and I had a great time at the factory, the latest equipments ran smooth and flawless, there ain't too much problems today as well ,only a few old machine malfunction" George said enthusiasticly, spooning his soup.

"That's great George, and you Rusty" Lucy asked him with a demured smile on her lips, She and George stared at Rusty intently, urging him to talk.

He let out a sigh of resignation but tried to smiled whole-heartedly, no , not whole-heartedly but almost whole-heartedly . "W ell...at least Sherley had fun"

"Is something wrong dear? " Lucy struck him with the most gentle stare.

"Not that it's wrong big time, but I... I just don't feel fun and happy when I'm with her, I don't get to make decisions decisions when she's around, even my preference on clothing she interferes, I just feel choked on the neck by her" he said finally letting it out.

"What's your plan? " George asked him quitly. Lowly and quitly almost in a whisper.

" nothing, just let her be I guess"he said spooning out his soup "but I really want to part with her"

Lucy reached for his hand and patted it. " dear, you made the decision to be with her, and only you could take it back, its your decision if you want to part with her"

"But what about the facfory?, the Company, the would terminate our partnership if I broke up with her"

"The factory managed to run ten years ago without the help of the Darrens, and now the factory is stable with or without them, this time think of your ow happiness dear, you have dedicated too much of your life in the factory already"

"Bu... But I.... I wanted keep my father's legacy, they raised me to run it, it's my Destiny"

"I'd that is your destiny, then I have no problems with it, no dear not at all, but I want you to find happiness too, you have lost your childhood earlier that most kids did, it breaks my heart to see you frustrated about things your not supposed to face until your older"

"I... I understand Lucy" he smiled at her, wiping the tears at the corner of his eye that wasn't there a moment earlier.

Lucy smiled back at him, she got up from her chair and walked towards Rusty, she placed a gebtle hug at Rusty' s back. " do what brings you happiness dear, the factory is stable now, don't worry about it too much"

"Yes Lucy" he knodded.

CHAPTER 12

"Good morning Mr. Luvré" Bella greeted Rusty as he entered the factory. Loud machinery buzzed and hummed on different pitches. "The Canoir brothers are waiting for you" she said loudly on his ears.

"At the office? " he asked just as loud, checking an old machine, the same corking machine his father assigned him more than ten years ago.

"No sir, they're at the parking"

"I'll be there in a sec" he said still investigating the machine. Bella knodded at him and turned. " oh and Bella, please fetch George for me, he's in my office. Tell him to meet me on the parking "

"Yes sir" Bella walked away towards his office as he walked out the factory.

He exited the factory, the air outside was cooler, the air inside wasnt hot at all but warm, warm enough to keep his people moving and comfortable. Peebles crackled under his boots, sliding sharply, popping as they did so, he wanted to remove the Peebles, but dicided against it, it prove usefull for car parking. He saw the Canoir's vehicle on thier usual park spot.

"Good Morrow Mr. Luvré" William exclaimed as Rusty approached them, flailing his arms in the air.

"hello Mr. William" he smiled back "Mr. Robert" he bowed at Robert.

"no one around.there is? " William wriggled his head around.

"Weird sentence, but none is around, yes" Robert answered looking around himself.

"Good" Rusty said " so, whatya call me for? " he asked the brothers.

"I'll leave today " robert said "I reckon I told you that? "

" yes you did" Rusty knodded.

"But I also want to take William today"

"But I'll leave today, I have plans for the big city, I was hoping to take George to drive me" he said ,but not in a tone of argument.

"I'm sorry but- "

"It's totally fine" Rusty said haistely.

"Great, thanks rusty, and oh! You can leave anyway Ive told Dolphy to supervise today, I may or may have not told her you're leaving too" said Robert.

"You have this all planned out, didn't you? " William punched Robert's shoulder playfully.

"Then you should get going" Rusty said to the both of them.

"We should" Robert said hopping into the car.

"Bye Rusty " William chuckled, opening the car's front door.

"Bye you two" He knodded at them while the engine started, hot dark fumes blew out the cars pipe .

"See ya later" Robert said, poking his head through the window, Rusty knodded at him, Robert strirred the car through and out the factory's parkway. He watched their car bobbed smaller and smaller.

"They've gone already?" He heard George behind him, he looked at George raising his brows giving the "yup" look.

George stared distantly, trying to catch a glimpse of the car, but it's nowhere near their sight. He turned to Rusty and said" so you called me? "

"Ah yes, could you drive me to the big city? "

"Of course"

"We'll be quick I just need to see Sherley"

George rolled his eyes dully at the mention of the name, Rusty stared at him questionably.

"Hop on, we don't want to keep her waiting"George opened the door for him.

Rusty did as told, hoping into the car, the leather cover of the seats squeaked at the slightest pressure. George ignited the engine, bringing it to life, roaring as it did so. The whole car vibrated as it advances towards the big city. Lucky for them since the last decade more roads connecting Rocco to the big city were built ,the travel time only last more or less than an hour. George stayed quiet as they drove through the outskirts of Rocco. Weird, Rusty thought, George was usually noisy when they drive, talking to William with the most nonsense of things, or laughing at Rustys incomprehensible hissis.

"George? "

"Hmmmm? "

"You'kay? " he asked him through the mirror.

"Oii!" George halted suddenly.

"what's happen? "

"A Hare, it hopped on the road, I almost ran over it" George said nervously, checking the road for more hares.

He resumed driving when he made sure there wasn't, the outskirts of Rocco melted before Rusty's eyes and was replaced with the towering buildings of the big city. Cars started to increase in numbers. The air turned noticeably hot and sticky, dust entered the half opened window. The car parked in front of a small tea shop, although the said shop also sells coffee.

Rusty looked around and there, he found Sherley, her pastel blue dress stands-out on the dusty murky salmon paint of the shop, he sighed staring at her through the glass wall of the shop.

"George she's inside, could you wait for me? I won't take long I just need to tell her something" he asked George as he stand under the hot sun rays, his blonde hair burned gold at the light ,his blue eyes sparked as he blinked, dazzled by the sun.

"Sure, I'll wait here "he said squeezing his eyes to somehow help his sight.

Rusty ran towards the shop's door, he grabbed the handle but stopped, he squeezed it rounding up his courage. Breathing very shallow he opened the door and walked straight to her.

"You're late! Where have you been? You wasted my five minutes ! I noticed you've been tardy lately! What is wrong with you?, if this continues we might as well break up" she babbled, her voice strong and sharp but lowered

"Yeah, might as well" he said lowly not meeting her gaze.

"What did you say?!" she asked ,her voice a bit louder.

"Look. Sherly" he started sighing not even bothering to take a seat. " for the past ten years, have you been really happy?, cause i feel you didn't ,when im around you're always high tempered, shouting at me, hitting me, controling me. That's not how relationships work, relationships operate on trust, respect and love "he met her eyes, establishing eye contact. " we have failed to have those " he finished.

"No! I love you Rusty" she argued

"No you don't, I'm just one of your blinging accessories, some-thing you can brag on your friends, your personal puppet to follow your orders, your pet that follows you around, your prisoner that you trapped on the chains of your fake love,its time we part ways"

"No ! You cant break up with me,or you'll lose your biggest client!" She treatened Rusty with her forefinger.

" the factory can run without your father's help" Rusty said turning back.

"You'll regret it Rusty!" Rusty heared her shout behind him " you'll crawl back to me begging"

Rusty took a swift sharp breath but didnt faced her,he released his breath and continued on the door,steping out the shop into the hot road towards the car where George is waiting for him.

"We need to leave quick" he said without halt,not waiting for George and opened the door himself. George sprinted towards him and slided inside the car,he turned the key and the engine roared to life.

"You did it finally?"George asked him carefully, as if it was the most fragile topic for a conversation.

"I...I did, Lucy made me see everything I ignored for the past years" Rusty whispered, afraid of the consequences of his actions.

George glanced at him and did nothing, just checked him from time to time.

It was a sunny day on Rocco, Rusty tended his factory like he always do,trying to forget what happened yesterday. He sat on his desk,shuffling the deck of papers on his hands. He tapped his finger tip on the desk rhythmically. Pursing his lips reading the papers swifly.   Suddenly, quite surprisingly a soft hurried knock vibrated from the door, that couldn't be Bella, she was for sure still doing her rounds.

"Come in"He said loudly.

The door clicked open with a ghastly sound. Robert came in, a smile present on his red face. His square jaw was clutched, but he knew all too well that that smile was authentic.

"Hi"he greeted Robert returning the smile.

"Hi, Rusty" he said, the smile suddenly vanished from his lips. "I need to make this fast, he might come in anytime " he said looking back at the door.

"Who?, William? "

"Yes, I want to invite you. I planned a small gathering for William at the mansion,tonight" Robert said without pause.

"Sure, tonight" Rusty repeated.

Robert smiled assured. "I wanted to-"

The door opened with a lively bang, George came in looking back at his shoulder, laughing. Behind him was William, brows crossed. His lips fell into a slant grim line. "I was kidding! " George stopped laughing when he noticed William's features. He threw his arms around William's shoulder and repeated "I was kidding" this time lower without the laughs. William hiss and sighed at the same time. He grunted in response and removed George's arm forcely.

"I'll expect you later" Robert whispered ,his face down "bring George with you to keep you company"

"I will" Rusty answered.

"Great " he said and turned back. Facing his brother. " now George, If you'll excuse us, I'll get this old man out of here" pulling William by the arm.

"Yes of course, please do" George said courtly , a playful smirk on his lips.

"Well, this old man is three years younger than you" William talked back, Rusty bit his lower tongue, a smirk growing on his own lips.

"How rude!" Robert said sourly.Rusty burst out in laughter, this old man teases, are a recurring joke between them, especially on the brothers.

"Now if you may, the young man here has work to do" George opened the door for them. The brothers stared at him with equal sourness.

"Mr. Rusty, I'll be with Mr. William, if you need something-" George said he himself about to exit the door.

"Yes George, but please with need to go home early today, I'm sure Mr. Robert do too" Rusty raised his head towards Robert.

"That is correct" he knodded at everyone.

As the three-George and the Canoirs made thier leave, Rusty returned to his papers, occasionally getting up from his desk to check his employees. Bella asked once or twice if he wanted coffee, which he kindly refused. The hours on the factory had thier own mind, there are times when they became too short that the work that needed to be done seemed too time consuming, while there are also times when they became too long that it seemed too little things to do-and this is one if these times. He had finished his paper works, but there is still an hour to spend. He dicided to go down his office and help corking the bottles, not that his help can make a difference, he just wanted to. He worked the bottles and observed the machines, until finally the clock struck time.

"George! Ready? " Rusty haistely asked poking his head inside George's room. "The Canoir car is outside "

"Already?!, you know you could have told me about this, then I don't have to strangle myself with this necktie" George said, muttering the last words.

"Need to go, hurry " Rusty said urging him to move faster.

"I AM IN A HURRY" George said forcefully giving-up on his crumpled tie.

They both half ran half walked out the room and to the kitchen, they kissed Lucy good-bye who smiled at them, admiring them from head to toe. They jogged outside the house and zooted to the cacky parked car.

"Good evening " Rusty greeted the driver as they climbed inside.

"Good evening sirs" replied the driver. Bowed.

The driver, reignited the car to life, It advaced smoothly through the dark night ,cold air fell on the ground, the moon peeking through the thin curtains of dark clouds, stars formed odd geometric shapes in the sky. Rusty noticed George struggling to find his peace.

"Its just a simple party, no biggi" Rusty assured him, tho he thought wierd of it, George is always a picture of grace, at least he is for Rusty, but this time he still is ,only his grace isn't as graceful as he always did.

"Yes, no biggi" George let out a nervous breath and smiled, his lips curled and crumbled, the crooked smile stayed on his lips.

"Hey George, you're acting absurd, you fine? " he asked determined to acquire an answer.

"Yeah, I'm fine" George said not meeting his eyes, he adjusted his position grunting as he did so.

"Then why act wierd? "

George swallowed, his eyes up ahead of them, "I might know the purpose of this party" he whispered, making sure the driver won't hear them.

"What? " Rusty asked in a whisper as well.

"You'll know eventually " George said aloud, he turned away from Rusty and stared into the nothingness outside the car window.

Rusty satred at the road ahead of them, they were getting nearer. The Canoirs live in a town called Humblemaynds, a town just beside Rocco, it's smaller in size but just the same condition as Rocco, Concrete roads stretched into a stone mansion that stood aglow amidst the creeping darkness, lampposts bordered the mansion's land. A small stage was set up in the front garden, he noticed william in there in his usual light coloured suit, But as the car approaches the mansion Rusty noticed he was wearing a faintly Grey colour.not his usually pale blue and silver.

The car finally stopped at the front garden, red carpet of heavy polyester served as the pathway towards the stage ,a number of meticulously crafted white small tables scattered evenly on the lawned grass beneath thier feet.

William greeted them with a smile. He walked haistely towards them. "Hi Rusty, George"

"Hello" Rusty greeted back, returning the half of his smile.

"Hi" George said, clutching his Jaw. His lips barely moved as the word came out of him.

"Let me show you your table" he motioned them to follow" we're expecting a few more guests ,it's best to find your own table, before the other people arrive" he pulled the small chairs that tucked under the white painted wooden table. "And George your tie is... " he stared at George and his tie, and to the darkness, thinking which word he'll use "lopsided " he finished.

A small smirk appeared at the corner of his lips " you notice everything , don't you? " ,George slowly untied his tie, "I... I was in a hurry" he said lying it around his neck.

"Let me-" William took the tie and pulled George closer, fixing it for him.

"Ohh there you are! " Robert shouted as he approach them " good evening you two" he said courtly.

"Good evening Robert" they chorused, knoding courtly.

Robert smiled at them and returned thier knods. "I wanted to check on you, we might start in a very few minutes" he said before leaving.

And as the few minutes passed, the party did start. The garden was full of lights it seemed it was in daylight. " Good evening everyone! " Robert greeted everyone " as all of you know it, as the letters of invitation said, William-my younger brother " he stared at William, everyone did so, " will marry someone from the guests "

Everyone knodded, but William was clearly surprised, his eyes stared at Robert with shock " no " he mouthed.

"I... Is this-? " Rusty turned to George.

"Yes" was the only word that came from him.

William sat beside them frozen, his fist were resting on his lap clutched, his stares towards Robert was sharp but at the same time helpless. He never moved only his eyes followed Robert as he make way through the maze of people to sit with them.

"Yo... You didn't" William muttered to Robert, his voice at the Brink of cracking.

"I wanted to find someone to take care of you, we are growing old ,in no time Marry and I will get married. I wont be able to care for you anymore" Robert said.

"I'll find someone in my own time, and I can perfectly care for myself" he argued but he sounded as if he was begging.

"You are getting old. William. It's time for you to settle down"

" don't tell me that I'm old. YOU ARE OLD." William said rather forcely. He left his seat and walked away, not turning back as he entered the mansion.

"C-could I follow him?, he might want someone to talk to" George asked lowly, as if afraid of his own words.

"Yes, yes George ,Please" Robert said knodding while massaging his temples.

George shooted up and made his way towards the mansion.

"I know good is all you wanted" Rusty said referring to Robert, but staring behind him to George as he slowly entered the mansion.

"Of course, but I-i know one day I need to leave, no one will care for him" he said palms on his face.

"Yes he will need someone, he'll find it eventually in his own time"

"But his time is so uncertain. He'll learn to love that someone he'll pick tonight anyway, that's how I'd did"

Rusty placed his shoulders on the table, "but Robert. You and William are different, he might have plans on his own. "

"I know, but his plans are faulty" Robert sighed. " he needs to find someone tonight either way" he glanced at the guests as they share drinks.

Rusty smiled at him surrendering. " you only want the best for him" he said calmly but as well flatly, Rusty poured wine on thier glasses and handed one to Robert. Robert sipped his while Rusty chugged his in one gulp. " you tend to your guests, I'll look for them "

"Yes please " Robert said getting up from seat, the wine glass on his hand.

Rusty raised from his seat, and took a deep breath, allowing the night's air to enter his lungs, he can taste the wine at the base of this tounge. He straightened his back and started walking, his steps were large in his rather calm pacing. He knoded at anyone he met his way, an old man with balding bair, a lady on her fifthty's maybe the mother of one of the quests, and a young man that offered him wine.

He reached the mansion. It was huge, even bigger than the manor. Tall white Marble pillars guarded it's walls. Heavely carved and smoothed railing lined at the viewing deck from the second floor. A similar white staircase was position at the very front. Rusty climbed it and reached the front doors which is wide open.

"Hello sir, good evening" a woman greeted him, she smiled at him wiping her hands on her white apron that turned yellow over time.

"Good evening to you as well" he bowed.

"Oh no!, sir ,do not " the woman stopped him, but Rusty did either way.

"I'm just a visitor, I should pay respects" he smiled, "could you please tell me where William is?, and George as well, he's the man with blonde hair. Robert sent me to find them"

"I saw Mr. William ran upstairs sir, Mr. George followed him shortly" the woman answered sweetly.

"Thank you very much, now please excuse me" he bowed again and turned towards another staircase, only this was made of shiny dark wood, red carpet flows down unto the floor like a waterfall of coarse blood.

"Of course sir" the woman said and left, to the back door, that Rusty knew leads to the kitchen.

He took the stairs and up he did. Sliding his palms over the smooth railing. His steps were muffled by the carpet ,but the carpet itself made sounds comparable to walking barefoot on sand.

He reached the second floor, orange light bulbs protruded from the walls casting their weak warm glow around it. He was walking through a weakly lit hallway, doors presenting themselves every ten steps or so of Rusty. He knocked on the third door. "William?

" he called but he lowered his voice, afraid he might disturb someone else. "William! " he called again but no response.

He walked to the next door. "George? " he called but still no response. He tried turning the knob but it was locked. He moved unto the next door.

Surprisingly the door was ajar. He pushed it a few millimeters open. Rusty peeked inside ,the room was poorly lit just like the outside. He can see a shelf full of books, he wasn't expecting much but he peeked at the opposite direction. There, he found William. incased inside George's embrace, William had George cornered on the wall. They were kissing but the sparkling tears on William's eyes were evedent.Thier kiss was slow, calm, and silent. George wrapped William tighter.They let go, George leaned on the wall while William panted.William took a long breath and scemed to recover , he pulled George closer to him, and wrapped him in his arms, George rested his head on William's,his eyes closed. A weak sad smile on his red lips.Rusty breathed heavy, he regretted it, this is the very reason why eavesdropping was never a good thing. He turned around and prepared to leave.

"R-rusty? " George said from the inside.

Cold crept through his spine, should he run?, no that is a vey bad idea. Should he act he heared nothing?, his mind panicked. HE panicked. No he wasn't supposed to eavesdrop.

"Rusty? " It was William's turn to ask. The door slowly swung open, William and George came out, they were both panting, their lips and cheeks were red, beads of Sweat formed on their foreheads, thier hair was so ruffled it's hard to believe they looked decent earlier.

"I-i was looking for you, Robert wanted.. Wanted....... "His eyes jumped back and forth into their faces.

"He wanted to.. You... You to come down" he gulped, biting his inner lip.

George moved closer and placed both of his hands on Rusty's shoulder"What did you see? "

"I-... I've, I've seen enough " he said.

William hissed and scratched his nape, "uhhh, Rusty I hope you don't get mad about thi-"

" no!, tottaly not, i'm-i'm not against it! "

George smiled and removed his hands on Rusty " thanks Rusty but there Is one more thing-"

"What?! "

" I've decided Robert needs to know, could you fetch him for us? " William clasped his hands together.

"yes,YES!, yes of course" and with that Rusty ran down the stairs like his life depended on it, wind brushed his skin, his heart beated rapidly.

He streached his neck looking around as soon as he reached the garden, He found Robert among many other men his age. Rusty groom himself and faked a small smile. Chest up he approached the men.

"Good evening gentlemen" he greeted.

"Good evening"the men greeted back.

"Could I borrow the dear Mr. Canoir for a moment? " He calmly asked everyone.

"Of course" one of them answered. Robert stood up as Rusty motioned him to walked with him into the mansion.

"Have you found him? " Robert asked lowly tilting his head towards Rusty.

"Yes, he's in a room at the second floor, but he wanted you to come" Rusty said struggling to keep his calm.

"After you then" Robert said, allowing Rusty to take the lead.

Rusty walked really quickly, paying quick glances at Robert to make sure he can keep up.

"Here" he flicked his head to the door, behind it was William and George.

Rusty knocked and said , " he's here"

The door creaked open and William poked his head out. "Come inside Robert, please " Robert obeyed and wordlessly brought hisself inside. "You too Rusty" Rusty haistely went inside before William shut the door and locked the knob.

"Yes William? " Robert asked.

"I have picked who I want to end up"

"Good who is it? " Robert walked towards the window and looked beneath him, where a group of girls sat in a circle, chatting, giggling.

"Not from them" William said, sliding his fingers through George's. "I love him Robert, and no matter what you do, I won't end up with anyone else except him"

"H.. How? "Robert stared at them perplexed.

"It just happened, and it HAD happened "William said, implying that Robert has no power over it.

"You love him" Robert asked William.

"Yes"

"You love him? " Robert asked George.

"Yes, I'm sorry I didn't mean to, it just-"

"That's all I needed to know"Robert said and smiled at them, he walked closer, face to face with George. George stared at him frozen. Robert patted his shoulder and moved to William, he cupped his cheeks as the smile grew larger into a smirk.

"Rusty, George, William. " Robert said capturing thier attention "the guests are expecting an answer by the end of the night, take may car and go home" he pulled out a key from his pocket and gave it to George. "Take William with you, and if it's okay let him stay there for a few days"

George knodded at him, his features all grim.

"Quick take the back door and go"

With that Rusty rushed to open the door and ran downstairs. Followed by William and George he opened the door the woman entered earlier. He waited for George and William to enter first before he did himself. He closed and locked the door to find them frozen. The woman saw them she also stood frozen, shocked by the sudden intrusion.

"S-sirs" she mumbled.

Rusty managed a smile and calmed himself, " hi ,we need to go"

The girl returned his smile and said "of course sir"

"But can you please don't tell anyone you saw us? "

"Yes, sure sir" the woman politely answered.

"Thank you very much, we need to go now" Rusty bowed and motioned them to run outside, he went first and opened the back door.

"Thank you so much Rachel " William said and hugged the woman.

They ran outside and hopped into the car. George started the engine and they bolted into the night ,into the darkness, as they themselves melt into darkness.

CHAPTER 13

"Tommy!, stop pestering uncle Rusty" Duke gently said to the child on Rusty's lap, his name was tommy- a two year old son of duke with his wife Grace, Rusty was his godfather, Rusty smiled as little Tommy rubbed his palms on his cheeks.

He was sitting on a small coffee table inside the bakery. The air smelled sweet and fluffy, warm and fuzzy, soft and bready. Rusty visited Duke's bakery for a contract signing, Duke wanted Rusty to supply his bakery with milk and cream.

"Okay Tommy, play with mum now, Dad and I has something to talk about"

"Tommy smiled and patted Rusty's cheek with his small hands.

Rusty slowly lifted Tommy up, Grace gently pulled him from Rusty. "He's not like this to others " Grace said eyeing rusty, she smiled rubbing Tommy's back.

"Well, that's flattering " Chuckled Rusty.

Grace carried Tommy away from him, they went back inside the back room where they bake their bread and pastries.

"Cute child" he said staring blankly on the door, as if he can see through it, as if he can still see tommy.

"That is why you need your own " Duke said taking the seat afront Rusty.

Rusty chuckled. A child of his own, he never really thought of it until now, Duke had started a family, and George and William - they are thier own family now, he might as well start making his own.

The door of the bakery opened, a bell chimed, as George and William entered. Arm in arm smiling thier hearts out.

"Finally the couple's here" Rusty stared at them from his seat.

"Are they? In lov-? " Duke asked also looking at them.

"Yep" George's and William's faces radiated with a warm glow, it was a glow that is unseen by the eye of someone that can't understand it, thier glow brought the sun with them, the bakery was showered in light. He saw that light once in his parents, but as he grew older, their light begun to dim that the last time Rusty saw them, the time before they died their light had completly vanished.

"Are we late already? " William asked lowly, swallowing his smile.

Rusty straightened his back and stiffined his voice, "very" he said in a very business-y way.

"I'm very sorry" George said apologetically.

"That is quite alright,please take your seats, now Mr. George the papers please"Rusty said keeping his formal character, business in business afterall.

"Here you are sir" George handed him the papers as he and William each took a chair and sat.

"Now Mr. Duke, please do sign here, here, and here" Rusty pointed out three different pages for Duke to sign in.

Duke signed as told and returned Rusty the papers completely signed and everything.

"Thank you, Mr. Duke, I'll personally see to it that you are provided with our highest quality products"

"Thank you " Duke smiled.

"It is nice doing business with you" Rusty gave Duke a copy of the contract and offered a hand which Duke Shook affectionately.

Rusty smiled finally, if only it was just a smile, it was a large grin.

"I cant believe you are that scumbag friend of mine ten years ago" Duke said his eyes were nostalgic. " not that it was bad you grew" he added fast.

Rusty chuckled "I am still that scumbag friend of yours"

" I know" Duke said lowly,laughing. "and by the way, couple aren't you?"Duke stood up from his chair and moved closer to William and George.

"Y-yeah" William said smiling shyly, his cheeks reddened.

It fascinates Rusty how love works. It is so unpredictable that it managed to bring them together, they that always contrasted each other, George was somehow younger but he acts more maturely, while William was older but he can be a bit childish sometimes. George likes to sit and read books while enjoying the calmness, William is loud ,energetic and adventurous.

"I see" Duke said aloud, "Grace!, we've got a couple here!, can you bring out a honey cake here?! " he shouted to his wife.

Grace came out with a jiggly pudding cake in a wodden tray, Tommy clinging at her long skirt. "Who? " she asked sweetly, looking around.

"Here " Duke patted thier shoulders.

"Ohhhhhhhhhhhhhhh" she squealled, she ran slowly towards them, tiptoeing as she did so but carefull enough not to let Tommy fall. "George! Finally! Ahhhhhhh" she squealled again.

"Yes Grace, finally " George said smiling, he reached for William's hands and laced his fingers through his. William blushed even more, he bit his lip and lowered his head.

"You complement each other" she said placing the tray on the table. Grace pinched her chin and abserved them in more detail, "actually no, you actually contrast each other. The hair ,you're blonde his is dark, the clothes , you wear dark he wears light"

"That's what I thought! " Rusty agreed.

"You still make cute couple either way" Grace said standing straight.

"You are always correct, hun" it was Duke's turn to agree.

Tommy climbed into William's lap as Grace sliced the cake. George stared at him jealous.

"Why? " William asked oblivious.

"Tommy never let George carry him" Grace said chuckling.

Rusty looked at William as Tommy tugs gently oh his curly hair.

"I need to go to... " he said to everyone "to.. You know, to take care of these papers, but I'll leave this two here"

" sure, but be sure to visit us again sometime" Duke said clapping his back.

"Of course " he said and kneeled down totommy "I'll visit everytime we deliver your orders, to see this young man right here" he pinched Tommy's nose playfully, Tommy laughed clapping his hands.

"But the car-" Said George.

"Will stay here for you, I'll find myself a carriage to bring me home" Rusty finished George's sentence for him.

"Yes Rusty" George said knowing he can't change his mind.

"I got to go now, goodbye everyone " he waved at them and pulled the bakery's door open.

The cool gentle wind of Rocco embraced him as he pushed himself out the shop, it was so gentle and soft no one would refuse it's hug. Copper skies stretched for a thousands miles above him, or maybe more, who knows?, no one. The afternoon sun shines golden at the lap of the skies, cradled by the thick clouds that floated in the sea of Amber glow.

Rusty reached a corner of the road, he stood beside an old lamppost and waved a carraige to pick him up. One if the carriages stopped in front of him, the driver courtly tapped the brim of his tattered hat while his dirty white stallion nickered, kicking the ground.

"Hello there, where are you headed? " the man asked.

"Hello" Rusty gretted the man as he climbed up the carriage. "To the luvré Manor past the hill please"

"Luvré Manor, of course" the driver said before flicking the small rope on his hands, sending the horse in a slow jog.

"I assume you are the son? " the driver asked without facing him "the last son that is"

"Yes" Rusty said, he tried to smile but his words rather came out flatly.

"I've heared you've-taken job to run the lo-local dairy, how come a bu-sy man like you ended up in the town?, alone at that. " the man's speech gets interrupted as the carriage bumped into the rough road.

"I have had a client to meet earlier, and my colleagues had other business to attend to" Rusty said simply, looking at the man's nape, his reddish hair curls under the tattered and patched up hat.

The man seemed to lost interest on him and focused on the road, making small noises as the carriage's wheels hit stones that protrude up from the ground. The carriage finally reached the yellow field, the Manor visible from not so far away. The ride turned noticably smoother as the grass carpeted their path, only the horse had seemed to slow down, the tall grass might be to blame. As the horse slowly tuggs the carraige out the sea of yellowish grass blades, the Manor crept closer and closer. The wild tall grass became greener, thinner, shorter, the carriage gained speed as it entered the manor's gate, the dirt made small noises as the wheels rolled over it.

"There you go sir, Manor past the hill" the driver said, smirking at him.

"Thank you for your service" he said handing the man five silver boneels.

"You paid too much sir" the man handed back three of it, but Rusty Shook his hand in the air, refusing it.

"Oh no, that's intended, buy this partner of yours a stack of hay or a bag of oats" Rusty said refering to the horse as he climbs down.

"Yes sir, I'll do it" the man said gladly.

Rusty knodded and chuckled. He strode into the front door as the carriage stirred and fled away. He knocked on the door and waited. Foot steps slowly grew louder approaching him, the door clicked as the knob turns to unlock the door.

"Dearie you're back already" Lucy said sweetly opening the door wider for him.

"Yes, the signing didn't took long"

"Where are George and William? "She asked looking behind him.

"I left them at Duke's, Grace was enjoying thier company "

"I see, now you wait. Im cooking roasted chicken for tonight. " Lucy said glancing at the kitchen.

"I'll help" Rusty offered and ran to the kitchen before even Lucy could decline.

Lucy chuckled ,suddenly looking more youthful.

"How can I help Lucy?" Rusty asked looking around the kitchen.

"Well, Rusty dear, I haven't made the stuffing yet, you could Peel and chop those" Lucy pointed at the bundle of carrots and potatoes that lies on the sink.

Rusty took off his velvet vest and hanged it on a rack, he then folded the sleeve of his white under shirt before peeling a specificly large potato.

"Oh dear me! " Lucy said, swatting the air with her hands. "I should've givin you an apron, you might get dirt on that shirt"

"But it's okay" Rusty said still peeling the potato.

"No it's not, potato stains are especially hard to get rid of" Lucy muttered ,handing rusty a folded apron the colour of pot ash and soot.

Rusty put it on and smiled widely at Lucy, "Right" she knodded at him "now back to work" she said facing away from him and scrubbed the chicken with lemon.

Rusty's hand begun to discolor and get sticky as the sap dried on his palms. Lucy hummed lowly behind him.

"Dear? " Lucy asked.

"Yes" he answered, occupied on his potatoes.

"How do you feel about George and William? "

Rusty stopped peeling the vegetable and looked back at his shoulder. "It's okay, I guess, I mean I'm happy they found love in each other. They both were like big brothers for me, it makes me happy to see them happy" said Rusty and continued to peel his third and last potato.

Lucy made a grunt of agreement. "And you?, what about your love status? "

"Were off" He said, getting started on his carrots.

"It's not want I want to know, but I'll take it" Lucy said and resumed her humming. Lucy always talk in riddles and poems, is that an effect of wisdom to a person?, would he be talking in riddle too when he grow old? If he'll be he hoped he'll be like Lucy.

Rusty finished peeling and mincing the vegetables, Lucy took it and made the stuffing. He watched as she poured it inside the hollow chicken and sewed it shut.

"What do we do now?"

"We play the waiting game child" Lucy calmly said as she puts the chicken inside the gas oven. "Go change dear, it won't take very long, supper's'll be ready before sundown"

Rusty glanced outside, it was beginning to darken, the sky is now a sea of red and crimson, thin curtains of clouds stained the sky , the low sun casted tangerine rays to the window, hitting Rusty's hair that burned in a rusty color, his face glow as it reflected the light, his eyes dark on first glance stared at the sun, it made his eyes dark brown.

"You got your mother's looks, Rusty" lucy said, her figers on her chin as she admires him.

Rusty moved closer to Lucy and incaged her in a gentle embrace. Lucy breathe lightly and patted his back. "Go change now dear" she said haistely, lowering her head to hide the growing tears on her eyes.

"Okay" he smiled and ran out the kitchen, up the wooden stairs and into his room.

Night crept closer until it finally arrived, the sky became dark, cradling a thousand if not a million stars as they twinkle like reflective gems clinging into a wall. He looked at the sky, the bright moon smiled back at him, his thoughts soared with the stars, humans find themselves so big but yet here they are , staring at the stars. Insignificant. While the stars are humble, they only shine and twinkle in thier own time, they respect balance and there they are, above everyone, away, claiming the vast emptiness of space.

"Rusty, George and William had arrived, we'll be eating dinner" Lucy said as she poked her head inside Rusty' s room.

"Yes" he said.

Lucy waited for him and together they climbed down the stairs.

"Had fun? " he asked when he found George and William already seated in the table.

"Yes" they said simultaneously.

Rusty smiled and took his seat. He played with his fingers as he waits for Lucy to take hers. She knodded at everyone ,cue that it's time for dinner. Rusty ate happily, obeserving everyone, he caught Lucy staring at the couple, hc acted he didn't, George and William purposly brushes thier elbows or hands everytime they reach for something but always widraws back quickly as if the touch of one another causes an electric shock. Rusty tried hard to subdue his laughter. William caught his eye and blushed heavely.

"L... Lucy? " he asked nervously, his shoulders were tensed as he locked his jaw. George stopped eating and stared at him.

"Yes dear? " Lucy said in her usual calm tone.

"I-I know, you are a mother figure towards Rusty and George" William reached for George's hand and place his own above George's, squeezing it tight. "I wa-wanted, wanted to ask person- ally and formally for your blessing, me and George are in love and I hope to spend the rest of my life with him"

Lucy sat down her untensil and looked sternly at the both of them. "Love is a gift that shouldn't be played with, love can make people do great things but love can be misleading too, your age now is the age where love is the purist-your youth but with youth comes foolishness" she said in an equally calm tone as in her previous words.

William and George exchanged glances , holding each other's hands. They looked at Lucy. "We'll be there by each other's side, to avoid foolishness " George said.

Lucy smiled and lowered her head as if she was about to take a bite. But instead said "Very well, I know you make each other happy and I won't be on your way towards your bliss"

George's and William's faces brightened. "Thanks lucy" both of them said.

It was a fun night, Thier love for each other seemed to grow stronger, Lucy's blessing seemed to give them more strength to take on the world and fight for their love. Rusty said good-bye to William and George when they reached George's room which was formerly Ben's. Rusty entered his own room and prepared for his well deserved slumber. He punched and Shook his pillow to soften it up, he pulled down the covers and collapsed on the matress face down. But a knock vibrated on the door.

"Please come in" he shouted, face still burried on his bed.

The door clicked open. "Rusty dear? " it was Lucy.

"Hmmm? " he answered not moving.

"I was cleaning earlier, and I saw this"

Rusty pushed his self up, apologetically staring at his pillow which he Invisioned crying. He looked at Lucy's hand. She was holding a small piece of a rectangular paper, he took it and examined it closely. It was a Polaroid, browned and washed away by time.

"Who was the girl? " Lucy asked.

"He stared at the polaroid closer, there was him, his young self smiling beside a girl with long wavy hair as if it captured the ways, her eyes were radiant even on the faded ink. Everything flashed before his eyes, he remembered that faithful night in an equally faithful summer.

"It's Dianne, she's Dianne!" He shouted looking at the paper.

"Dianne?" Lucy asked.

"I need to return to mortiana, I promised. SHE PROMISED!"

CHAPTER 14

"Got everything? " George asked as he handed Rusty a leather bag.

"I suppose" Mumbled Rusty, checking the list of things he'll need in his mind.

After all this time, Rusty finally remembered. Ten years ago when he was just a young lad he ran away and ended up in mortiana, a coastal city hundreds if not thousand miles away from Rocco. He met Dianne, the most unusual girl he ever met, unusual in a very beautiful way. The tragic events that destiny poured over him became his hindrance and obstacle towards fulfilling his promise, he promised to come back, she promised to wait.

"Be careful there Rusty dear" Lucy said squeezing his hands.

"Yes lucy" Rusty planted a kiss on Lucy's cheek and smiled at her assuringly. He turned his gaze towards the trio of men beside her. Robert, George and William looked back at him.

"George please take care of Lucy while I'm gone"

"Of course " George grinned.

"And Robert, please do take care of the dairy, new machineries will be arriving this week, and some of our supplies are running low, we need to replenish it the soonest" He added, looking stern-ly at Robert.

"Yes, yes Rusty" Robert knodded keeping a calm face.

"Please take care of the factory you three"

Everyone knodded at him. "Go and find her already" William said pushing him up the platform.

"Yes I will find her, and just so you know, it's all your fault I'm going through this much trouble" he joked knowing it wasn't true at all, he himself deeply wanted to meet Dianne again. "You all had special someones ,I don't want to be left out"

They laughed, George wrapped his arms on William's waist from the back, placing his chin on William's shoulder. Robert glanced at them with smiling eyes.

Rusty climbed the train, steam covered the platform with clouds of hot white smoke, "where you up sir? " a stout man with short brown hair asked rusty, he was holding a stack of greyish-brown paper which are the tickets and a puncher.

"To the coast of Mortiana please "he said taking his seat, he placed his leather bag up his lap.

"Mortiana huh? " the man mumbled.

"Why? " rusty asked suspiciously.

"Not a lot of folks from the city goes there, it's been maybe a year since someone took a train to Mortiana " said the man, making holes on the ticket.

"I'm visiting a friend there"

"Mortiana is so far, how dya got a friend from there?" Asked the man handing him the ticket, "six boneels"

"I've been there once " Rusty shoved his hands on his pockets and pulled out six silver coins handing it to the ticket man.

"I see, well enjoy your trip" the man flicked his fingers on his forehead, casting Rusty a playful salute .

Rusty knodded at him "thanks"

Few more passengers boarded the train. Not long after, the train whistled. It's whistle is so ear wrecking and high pitched. He waved goodbye to Lucy and everyone through the glass window. They waved back at him smiling.

The train's pistons started pounding, slowly moving the heavy wheels with every pump, each pump builds up speed, until the tain crawled slowly on it's tracks like a large metal snake, giving off white smoke as it slithers. The train did gained speed and shooted away, Rusty watched as Rocco passed through his eyes like a blurr of different colours, his heart beated hevealy, finally, after all these years, he is back, just wait a little bit more Dianne. He'll be back by your side.

The train traveled like a drop of rain, fast and almost unstoppable. The sun traveled with it and slowly ,it got tired and sunked lower in the skies. When the train finally reaches Rocco, the day was already bleeding, skies were painted red as thin threads of clouds floated in it, a subtle twinkle of stars can already be seen making faint maps on the Ruby sky. He looked around, mortiana had changed.

Rusty climbed down the train, stepping into the dusty station. It seemed new, pillars stood at the sides, freshly coloured with green paint. He stepped on the dusty floor, dirt sticking to his shoes. An officer in a navy shirt and shorts walked passed him.

"Excuse me officer" he halted him, "are the rental cabins by the shore still there? "

"Yes, it's been quite lively lately, many guest from Carreitte city fleed into here" the officer answered, Rusty never heared of Carriette city before.

"Carriette? " he asked oblivious.

"Yes, the city " the officer answered patiently.

"Never heared of it before, I'm from Rocco"

"Oh, you're from the other end" the officer said bobbing his head, "the terrorists reached Carriette, the war had been going on for weeks. Let's hope they never get here" , the officer added.

"Can can I know the directions to the cabins sir? " Rusty asked not wanting to dive deeper unto the current subject.

"Oh yes, take this road" the officer waved forward into a road full of tall tenements. "It's a couple minutes walk, when you hit the end you'll see the school, take a turn and walk straight ahead until you reach the inn, from there you'll see the beach"

"Thank you kindly, officer" Rusty bowed. The officer tipped his hat and walked away.

Rusty did as told, he walked on the pavement beside the stacks of dark concrete tenements, the dying sun showered it in Ruby light, soaking it in red hue. He noticed the car had increased in numbers while the carriages did the other way. There are still groups of gossiping women by the corners, Rusty smiled to himself, it was something he is familiar with. He finally reached the inn. It radiated faint tangerene lights, it has the same glass front wall and the same roof tiles. A man was inside, wiping the tables, his back arched in a blunt curve, it wasn't the same man though. He walked past the inn and headed to the beach, he was greeted by the salty breeze blowing on his hair, the salty air entered his lungs, warm and heavy to take in.

Rusty reached the mossed stairway descending into the beach, he carefully tackled it down step by step, until he reached the cluster of cabins. The cabins themselves seemed to multiply as it is noticably more than he remembered. He walked towards the biggest cabin,the one with the red tiled roof. He knocked gently ,waiting for someone to open it.

Loud thuds came from inside ,the door open energitically,the smell of alcohol and tea hugged his nose. A large man sporting a firey mane of long matted hair, appeared, rusty noticed the white streaks of his hair at the sides of his head.

"Good evening" Rowlin greeted.

"Good evening I am looking for Rowlin" Rusty greeted back.

"That would be me, how can I be of help? "

Rusty smiled and allowed his face to be bathed in light. "Its me, Rusty"

Rowlin's eyes widened ,a large feline grin appeared on his mouth. "Rusty?, is that really you? " he opened the door wider. "Come in, come in"

Rusty walked inside, looking around. Rowlin's cabin in now full of ornaments, big sofas draped in maroon velvet. A half empty bottle of gin stood on a small square table. "Have a seat please" Rowlin offered a big sofa. Rusty sat on it comfortably.

"How are you Rowlin? "

"Oh fine, good really, I used the money you gave me to pay thildy, without my debt I manage to save money and improve my rental business, and it is all thanks to you Rusty"

Rusty grinned at him, not wanting Rowlin to press on deeper.

"Wow, just wow, you came back, for how long?" Rowlin asked smiling.

"That's up for destiny to decide" rusty smiled back, "and for that, I need a place to stay in,can I have the same cabin?"

Rowlin's smile faded, "oh that, it was destroyed by the storm, and I can't offer you any room, my cabin's all rented. Since the war, people come here to seek refuge and peace, some rented those filthy tenements, some ended up here"

"What should I do now?, I don't have room to sleep, the inn might be full too" Rusty scratched his nape.

"On the contrary, the inn has a room, their rooms are too small for a family. I'll walk you there" Rowlin offered ,rising from his chair, time might have whitened his hair, but it didn't managed to affect his stance. He still stood proud and high. Rowlin pulled up Rusty's leather bag and carried it on one shoulder.

"I can carry that-" Rusty tugged lightly on the bag but Rowlin didn't budged.

"I'll walk you there rusty" Rowlin repeated smiling timidly at him.

As they opened the door they were greeted by darkness, rusty was sure their conversation didn't took too long. But the sky were now dark blue, stars spetacled the dark sea of emptiness like thousand of beating heart, shining in thier own colours, twinkling on thier pace, being themselves as for who they really are.

"Everything had changed" Rusty said as he stared at the lights of the tall tenements that swarmed mortiana, his voice echoed through the cold air, a weak gust kissed him, hugging his face, caressing his lashes as he fluters it.

"The only constant thing in this world youn-" Rowlin scoofed, "Rusty, is change" Rowlin said heavely, eyes ahead of them. "I almost called you young Rusty, but you're a grown up man now, see? you also did changed " Rowlin laughed, casting a quick glance at him.

Rowlin could be right, he might have changed himself, only it was very slow he didn't noticed it happening. "I might have grown, but I'm still that lad you met ten years ago"

Rowlin looked at him, " yes I still see that lad in you, but there is someone else, it's a serious young adult dressed in a professional manner, let me tell you this rusty." Rowlin breathe long.

"Young rusty. I don't know what happened to you over the years, but I see your inner child dying, the child in you is a part of who you are, don't let him die, if he dies, a part of your life dies with him. Your childhood. Never let him go, not all people still has their child in them, they're that people that had lost themselves"

Rusty knew what Rowlin meant but didn't at the same time, idiotic in other words.

"I-i never really thought about it, thanks for reminding me" he said truthfully. "I know the child in me wanted someone, my adult self wants the same"

"Someone? " Rowlin said, his low voice growled with the wind.

"Dianne" Rusty looked at Rowlin, but Rowlin still faced the road, they are getting closer to the inn, "how is she?".

Rowlin chuckled and Shook his shoulders. " she's great!, she's peaceful" he said, opening the door and getting inside the inn rather quickly.

"Joey?! " he shouted at the counter.

"What Rowlin? It's late" a tall old man appeared from the back door.

"We got guest" Rowlin stared at Rusty, Joey did too, Rusty gave him a smile which joey returned with an akward twitch of his lips

"He needs a room, I'll take his bag upstairs " Rowlin said and climbed the wooden stairs that led to the second floor.

"How long would you like to stay sir? " joey asked behind the counter.

"I still don't know yet" Rusty titlted his head, preparing himself to be shouted at by the man.

"Well then, for now you can pay for two nights, then if you decide to stay for longer we'll just add another two nights" Joey said calmly, drawing circles on the wooden counter with his finger tip.

"That's brilliant, I'll pay for the first couple of days" he said, thankful the man was so calm.

"Very well, that would cost sixteen boneels"

Rusty dug out his pocket for his leather wallet. He pulled out a pair of gold Shellies and slided it towards Joey, joey picked it up and opened the cash register. Pushing back four silver boneels.

" you're on room six Rusty" Rowlin shouted as he jogs down the stairs. "I need to go now, it's late" he said haistely waving at Rusty and jolted out the inn.

"Room six sir, please enjoy your stay " joey said without meeting his gaze.

"Thank you" he said shaking the coins inside his fist. " uhhm, what can get for these?, I don't want a really heavy meal" he said showing the four coins on his hands.

"You can get a bowl of vegetables with that"

"Great I'll have it" He slided the coins towards joey, he picked it up and dropped it in the cash register.

"Would you mind waiting sir?, I need to prepare your meal"

"No at all, in fact would you mind waiting for me?, I'd like to take a walk"

"No sir, please do take your walk"

"Thank you" Rusty said before jogging out the inn, his heart raised beats, he is about to meet her. On the mossy stairs, he stopped to take off his leather shoes, it is too uncomfortable to run with. With his shoes clutched on his armpits he jumped down the mossy stairs, sand tickled his sole, he ran towards the shore tracing it. The air was starting to cool down but the sand remained warm. He run beside the sea, the tall grass he remembered was still there, he smiled at the sight. Huffing as he bobbed up and down. Rusty knew he was getting closer to Dianne's cabin. As he ran closer he noticed a field of bay hops and coastal wall flowers on the beach, a new refreshing sight to see, the wallflowers stood out on the darkness, yellow against the blackness of the night, the same couldn't be said to the bayhops, it's light purple flowers were so demured, it didn't even bothered to stand out. He picked one of the bayhops, it reminded him greatly of Dianne, she was never proud, but she was always beautiful.

He continued to run towards the cabin, he can see it now. Its silhouette. A high pitched song rung on his ears,like the sea itself was making the melody."Dianne" he whispered loudly, ironic as it sounds it's what he did.

He pushed the wooden gate open, without stopping, running around the cabin towards the back pier. She was there.

Her back against him, her long black hair waved as the breeze blew on it, her dress the colour of the mist hugged her body ,flowing down her body like a calm waterfall.

"Dianne? "He said.

She turned to him wide eyed. "Rusty? Is that really you? " she ran towards Rusty and pulled him into a tight embrace. Rusty gently pushed her away and cupped her cheeks, they met eyes he can see the stars throught her brown gazes, he can see his whole world revolve around them, his whole life flashing within. He pressed his lips on hers. Her lips were so soft and warm, his whole body radiated with warthm. Rusty pulled his lips away from hers breaking the kiss.

"I should have done that a long time ago" he said catching his breath.

"You should have" she muttered smiling, her palms squeezed the gold ring that hangs in her neck she pushed it deeper to her heart. Tears trickled down her pale face. She collapsed on his chest sobbing. "I kept my promise Rusty, i waited for you" she said sobbing.

Rusty held her by the shoulder and placed a kiss on her forehead. "Thank you for waiting for me, im sorry I took too long to fulfill my promise"

Dianne stood up straight, Rusty cupped her cheeks and wiped the tears on her eyes. She smiled at him sniffing.

"It's late ,had dinner yet? "He asked her. Looking distantly at the sea.

Dianne shook her head modestly, her white dress flowing together with her movements. Rusty took a net and threw it in the water. "Ive learned a few things when i was away"

Rusty sat on the pier, resting his elbows on his knees, Dianne sat beside him resting her head on his shoulder. She lift his pant leg and traced a white scar on his calf. Rusty looked at his leg shocked he never really paid much attention to his leg since he became CEO of the dairy, he had lost so much of his time.

Dianne begun singing, her sirenish voice shook every star as it vibrated through the air, erriely alluring and beautiful. Fish hynotically swam towards the net ,entangling themselves. Soon enough their net was full.

Rusty hauled thier catch. He picked two of the largest fish and returned the others back to the water where they belong. "I hope you're not planning to give Willy some" he said looking at the fishes that swam in circles on a metal bucket.

Dianne grinned at him. "No im not"

"Shall we cook it then? " Rusty asked ,Dianne knodded vigorously.

She arched to pick up Rusty's shoes while he carried the bucket on one hand. He reached for Dianne's hand by the other. They entered the cabin, it was exactly as Rusty remembered it, the old wooden chest still stood in the corner, the cabinet ,the fireplace.

Rusty cleaned and cooked the fish over the crackling fire on the fireplace, it danced as it burned up and down. It bites the bottom of the blackened pot like a hungry monster hungry enough to eat everything. It casted warm orange light on their faces, playing with the shadows on thier features, distorting thier silhouettes in every crack of the flame.

Not too long after, dinner is ready. Rusty laddled the fish stew, Dianne handed him the bowls, he transfered the steaming hot stew in it. Dianne and Rusty crounched on the floor as they sip the stew, looking at each other. Happy with everything they have at the present moment.

"Rusty? " Dianne asked after they're done eating.

"Hmmm?"

"I want you to promise me something" Dianne reached for his hand and wrapped it with both of hers.

"Yeah, sure. Everything." He caressed her cheek with his thumb.

"Please do not visit me or my cabin during the day" She said, drowning him with her stares.

"But, w-why? " He asked.

"Promise me Rusty" she held his hands tighter.

"Yes, I promise" Rusty locked eyes with her to tell her he meant it, he was weirded out of course, but he had made his promise. Dianne smiled.

"Thank you Rusty"

CHAPTER 15

Cars roared passed him. Some dirty, some dirtier. The leisurely walk Rusty had enjoyed when he was young was nothing more but a busy and Dusty stroll. Mortiana had changed over the years. Some of the tall stacked houses were replaced by narrow tenements if not a small Villa.

The cobbled road he had once walked was replaced by concrete. Carriages had lessened in numbers while cars took over dominantly.

He walked slowly, studying everything his eyes can reach. He breath slowly, inhaling the air of Mortiana. Rusty looked around, he knew it was here somewhere. Tony's grocery should be here if his memory served him right.

He grinned when his eye caught the old grocery, still shabby and dusty. Sitting between two Villas ,that contrasting to it was in perfect condition, fresh white paint has hued the wall. Rusty peeked through the glass window. It was dark only the first aisle was visible.

Rusty pushed the door open. The air inside the shop was moldy and damp, crispy but sticky to breath in as it brushed his throat. Light didn't managed to sip through the glass window over the thick layers of dust that might have accumulated over the years. He moved carefully, taking effort not to make any noise or touch the dust covered products. As he walked deeper and deeper into the heart of the shop, the air turned more moldy, he had to stop several sneezes.

"What do you want? " a growly voice asked him, the voice made Rusty jolt into a stiff straight stance. He turned around and saw Willy, his watery eyes reflected the faint light of the shop. His large dark hands rolled into a loose ball.

"I... I was just checking in"

Willy growled and grasped his shoulders, His fingertips burrowed dully on Rusty's skin. "I know you" his said lowly, his breath smelled like alcohol. Willy pulled Rusty into the counter, banging him to the wall lightly, Rusty didn't know if it's his bones or his just hearing things because of fear, but he swear he heard something broke.

Rusty panted fast. Looking into Willy's eyes. He stared back at Rusty like he was about to tear him apart. "I know you, you're the boy! "

"How long have you been here?,what have you seen?, what are you doing here?!, have you seen her? " Willy bombarded him with questions.

"I... I, no.. What? " Rusty struggled to find his words.

Willy greeted his teeth, and squeezed Rusty's shoulder even more, His shoulder burned as Willy's finger stab his skin. Willy held him by the collar and pulled him harshly towards the door. Rusty's chest was pounding not knowing What would he do.

Willy tugged the door forcefully like he doesn't care if he'll broke it and threw Rusty out his shop. "Beware, she isn't what you believe, nor it is what you see" Willy pionted at him with a finger. "

go home and leave this place! " he riddled before closing the door with a loud bang.

Rusty swallowed . He bolted into a run, He heard Willy pick up something from the inside, it might be a gun, and he is good with guns, he was a soldier. He immediately broke into a run, knowing it's the best decision on his life. Yet.

Beads forming on his forehead, he tackled the shore, his shadow hit the ground like a deformed humaniod figure from the depths of hell.

The sun was starting to sink on the sea, the water had turned gold and red, small waves disturbed the distant horizon.

He was running out of breath but he didn't care ,all he wanted was to reach Dianne. Rusty's calves started trembling but it doesn't matter, he can see the cabin now.

He ran towards the gate and into the cabin, he collapsed on the floor catching his breath.

There were footsteps on the back pier coming towards him. Then a small demured laughter.

"What happened to you? ,you look.... Dismantled"

Rusty struggled to get up, pushing his body up with his shaking arms.

"Willy""Tried""To""Kill""Me" he said between breaths. Rusty looked at Dianne, her hair braided with a white satin ribbon hanged down her chest, the golden ring glistening under the faint glow of the sinking sun.

"Yeah, he can be a lunatic sometimes " Dianne sat beside him, stroking his hair.

"He doesn't like me, he never liked me Dianne! " he exclaimed, defeated.

Dianne chuckled and pushes his hair back up ."we aren't sure" She kissed his forehead and pulled him up.

Rusty limply grabbed onto her as she tugged him upwards. "Walk with me"

Rusty breathe in slowly and smiled at her, wrapping his arms around her waist. He kicked his shoe off his foot and carried himself and Dianne out the cabin.

The sea turned calm as they walked beside it, A small cresent moon sat above the skies,slowly waning to start anew. Waves kissed thier soles as the breezed embraced them.

Dianne smootched his cheek and giggled. " catch me if you can rusty" she shouted playfully as she run along the beach . Her flowery scent blessed Rusty's nose ,carried by the weak evening wind.

Rusty chased her ,his foot sinking on the wet sand. Dianne hopped around him ,as he run in circles panting for breath. He reached Diannes hand and they both fell on the water. Small slow waves swallowed thier hair, warm water running down thier faces. Dianne wiped her face with her palms laughing, Rusty pulled him into an embraced and kissed her. The sea ,the cresent moon, and the stars were witnesses of thier love.

They rised from the water held hands, Dianne resting her head on Rusty's shoulder, while he struck her with the warmest eyes.

They reached dry beach, bayhops covered the surface. Purple flowers adorned the green vines that formed dunes. Dianne collapsed on the plants and pulled Rusty with her. Laughing thier hearts out. Rusty covered her with his arms as they stare at the stars twinkling above them. Rusty wished he could pluck one of them and give it to Dianne.

Dianned traced his nose with her fingers that slowly slid down his lips, she placed her head on his chest as they breathed slowly. Sharing each other's warmth under the mysteriously beautiful skies.

"I love you Dianne, I love you now, I loved you ten years ago"
Diannes chuckled and pinched his nose, biting her lips smiling.

CHAPTER 16

Cars roared passed him. Some dirty, some dirtier. The leisurely walk Rusty had enjoyed when he was young was nothing more but a busy and Dusty stroll. Mortiana had changed over the years. Some of the tall stacked houses were replaced by narrow tenements if not a small Villa.

The cobbled road he had once walked was replaced by concrete. Carriages had lessened in numbers while cars took over dominantly.

He walked slowly, studying everything his eyes can reach. He breath slowly, inhaling the air of Mortiana. Rusty looked around, he knew it was here somewhere. Tony's grocery should be here if his memory served him right.

He grinned when his eye caught the old grocery, still shabby and dusty. Sitting between two Villas ,that contrasting to it was in perfect condition, fresh white paint has hued the wall. Rusty peeked through the glass window. It was dark only the first aisle was visible.

Rusty pushed the door open. The air inside the shop was moldy and damp, crispy but sticky to breath in as it brushed his throat. Light didn't managed to sip through the glass window over the thick layers of dust that might have accumulated over the years. He moved carefully, taking effort not to make any noise or touch the dust covered products. As he walked deeper and deeper into the heart of the shop, the air turned more moldy, he had to stop several sneezes.

"What do you want? " a growly voice asked him, the voice made Rusty jolt into a stiff straight stance. He turned around and saw Willy, his watery eyes reflected the faint light of the shop. His large dark hands rolled into a loose ball.

"I... I was just checking in"

Willy growled and grasped his shoulders, His fingertips burrowed dully on Rusty's skin. "I know you" his said lowly, his breath smelled like alcohol. Willy pulled Rusty into the counter, banging him to the wall lightly, Rusty didn't know if it's his bones or his just hearing things because of fear, but he swear he heard something broke.

Rusty panted fast. Looking into Willy's eyes. He stared back at Rusty like he was about to tear him apart. "I know you, you're the boy! "

"How long have you been here?,what have you seen?, what are you doing here?!, have you seen her? " Willy bombarded him with questions.

"I... I, no.. What? " Rusty struggled to find his words.

Willy greeted his teeth, and squeezed Rusty's shoulder even more, His shoulder burned as Willy's finger stab his skin. Willy held him by the collar and pulled him harshly towards the door. Rusty's chest was pounding not knowing What would he do.

Willy tugged the door forcefully like he doesn't care if he'll broke it and threw Rusty out his shop. "Beware, she isn't what you believe, nor it is what you see" Willy pionted at him with a finger. "

go home and leave this place! " he riddled before closing the door with a loud bang.

Rusty swallowed . He bolted into a run, He heard Willy pick up something from the inside, it might be a gun, and he is good with guns, he was a soldier. He immediately broke into a run, knowing it's the best decision on his life. Yet.

Beads forming on his forehead, he tackled the shore, his shadow hit the ground like a deformed humaniod figure from the depths of hell.

The sun was starting to sink on the sea, the water had turned gold and red, small waves disturbed the distant horizon.

He was running out of breath but he didn't care ,all he wanted was to reach Dianne. Rusty's calves started trembling but it doesn't matter, he can see the cabin now.

He ran towards the gate and into the cabin, he collapsed on the floor catching his breath.

There were footsteps on the back pier coming towards him. Then a small demured laughter.

"What happened to you? ,you look.... Dismantled"

Rusty struggled to get up, pushing his body up with his shaking arms.

"Willy" "Tried" "To" "Kill" "Me" he said between breaths. Rusty looked at Dianne, her hair braided with a white satin ribbon hanged down her chest, the golden ring glistening under the faint glow of the sinking sun.

"Yeah, he can be a lunatic sometimes " Dianne sat beside him, stroking his hair.

"He doesn't like me, he never liked me Dianne! " he exclaimed, defeated.

Dianne chuckled and pushes his hair back up ."we aren't sure" She kissed his forehead and pulled him up.

Rusty limply grabbed onto her as she tugged him upwards. "Walk with me"

Rusty breathe in slowly and smiled at her, wrapping his arms around her waist. He kicked his shoe off his foot and carried himself and Dianne out the cabin.

The sea turned calm as they walked beside it, A small cresent moon sat above the skies,slowly waning to start anew. Waves kissed thier soles as the breezed embraced them.

Dianne smootched his cheek and giggled. " catch me if you can rusty" she shouted playfully as she run along the beach . Her flowery scent blessed Rusty's nose ,carried by the weak evening wind.

Rusty chased her ,his foot sinking on the wet sand. Dianne hopped around him ,as he run in circles panting for breath. He reached Diannes hand and they both fell on the water. Small slow waves swallowed thier hair, warm water running down thier faces. Dianne wiped her face with her palms laughing, Rusty pulled him into an embraced and kissed her. The sea ,the cresent moon, and the stars were witnesses of thier love.

They rised from the water held hands, Dianne resting her head on Rusty's shoulder, while he struck her with the warmest eyes.

They reached dry beach, bayhops covered the surface. Purple flowers adorned the green vines that formed dunes. Dianne collapsed on the plants and pulled Rusty with her. Laughing thier hearts out. Rusty covered her with his arms as they stare at the stars twinkling above them. Rusty wished he could pluck one of them and give it to Dianne.

Dianned traced his nose with her fingers that slowly slid down his lips, she placed her head on his chest as they breathed slowly. Sharing each other's warmth under the mysteriously beautiful skies.

"I love you Dianne, I love you now, I loved you ten years ago"

Dianne chuckled and pinched his nose, biting her lips as she smiles at him.

CHAPTER 17

"Hello?, Rowlin? Are you there? " Rusty was knocking on Rowlin's cabin, he never saw Rowlin once since he walked him to the inn. Maybe he's working at the inn already, he thought and ran back up the mossy stairs.

It was one of the rare days of summer. Thick dark clouds hovered on the skies, the sky itself was gray and gloomy. The sun, although shining isn't too happy either, weak pins of light struck mortiana trough the holes in the sky the clouds havent been able to cover. The wind was warm and sticky, It wrapped Rusty's whole body into an uncomfortable embrace.

Rusty reached the inn, it's yellowish walls stand aglow and shiny under scarce light. Looking from the outside, rusty saw the inn was already busy, people had arrived for thier breakfast chattering and chirping like a flock of sparrows. He gently opened the door and poked himself in.

"Excuse me, have you seen rowlin? " he asked the old man that tends the counter.

"Didn't sir, he asked for a leave the other day" the man said wiping a clean glass mug with an even cleaner towel.

"Oh? " Rusty grunted, where could Rowlin be?

"I'm sure, he's on one of his manly expeditions" said a woman in a frilly gown, her hair was tied all up by pins, her cheeks round and red like beets, lips that pouts lopsidedly.

"Why are you looking for the man anyway?" The voice she held risen Rusty's blood, he never liked thildy, not ten years ago not now. Thildy hasn't changed that much, she is still proud, she still wore her frilly dress that made look like a dismembered peacock. Though more lines had appeared on her face, which Rusty could see she tried hard to hide, her thick make up didn't help at all of course.

"I am a friend " he said calmly, mastering a smile .

Thildy stared at him, completely unbelieving, " you look like a man of fortune, how can you be friend with that matted hair ball? ", she laughed, Rusty gritted his teeth and hid it with a smile.

He was about to turn and leave, away from Thildy, he was trying hard not to burst out.

"Please sir, sit with me" Thildy patted the table, Rusty thought to refuse her.

"No thank-"

Thildy pulled him by the arm and slammed him to his seat, opposite to hers, at least he is not siting beside her, he thought.

"What are you here for? " she asked, her yellowish teeth peeking through her red lips.

"I'm here to-"

"Looking for a bride aren't you?" Thildy didn't let him finish, clearly she wanted to do the talking.

"I kind of-" Thlidy cutted him again.

"Of course you are, now lucky for you I am a match maker, for a fee of course, I can get you the best girl"

"No, I-"

"I'll only get a girl from a wealthy family of course, we don't want a filthy girl. Uneducated, doesn't dress formally, poor" why is she like this?, why is she so mean?,

He breathed heavily and rose from his seat "No, thank you, if those wealthy girls are like you, I'd rather grow old alone"

Thildy looked at him shock, her eyes widened, her lips pursed. her throat wiggled as if she was to say something. Rusty turned back at her and left. Heat coursing through his veins. His temples prickled as he squeeze his knuckles tight. All while haistely walking out the inn.

"Where are you Rowlin?! " he whispered in the air, clutching his teeth. He looked around hoping to catch sight of him. But Rowlin disappeared without any trace, as if he wiped himself off out of existence.

Rather gloomy ,Rusty proceeded back to the cluster of cabins. It had grew into a small village, as rusty saw it. There could be thirty cabins now, standing at the shore. Facing in all directions, they had the same plane windows, same narrow wooden doors, but different coloured wood walls, others were reddish in hue while others seems rather dark. A thin forest of mangroves had grew at the back of the cabins ,thier roots scattered on the sand like a complex network of minature bridges, canopys of green foliage ornated the thin ,oddly shaped branches. It swayed gracefully, rustling quietly as a weak sea breeze approach the shore, it played with Rusty's hair. Ruffling it ever so lovingly.

The cool touch of wind, soothed him, releasing the anger for Thildy he had in his chest with every blow. He mastered a small smile and stared at the horizon.

He looked at the sky, the gray clouds seemed to melt from the skies, it was now sunny as it's supposed to be. A thin line of blue separated the water from the sky, if not for that thin line, the water and sky could be one. The sea burned silver under the sun, while the sky radiated blue, even brighter than the sea.

Rusty sat on the beach, sand pushed through the gaps of his fingers as he settles his hand on the ground. He can feel the heat on his buttoms. Sweat beaded on his forehead as sunlight kissed his whole body.

Rusty carefully, removed his shoes, stretching his toes afterward.

Clutching the leather shoes at the pit of his arms, Rusty walked along the shore. Waves playfully nibbled on his toes, sand sticking to his pants. He walked on the shore kicking the water lightly.

He didn't noticed but he had walked too far. The cabins were gone, and he can sea the feild of coastal flowers not so far away. Yellow dots adorned the biege beach. He ran closer, the wallflowers burned yellow brightly. Rusty picked a few flowers to make a small boque . He ran next to the bayhops, which was blooming with thier purple flowers. His smile grew even wider. Rusty carefully picked few bayhop blossoms and added it the flower bundle on his hand.

"Promise me" Dianne's voice rung on his ear.

Rusty stared at the flowers in his hand, he really wanted to give it to her, they are more beautiful in daylight. He grunted. He can't broke his promise. He promised not to visit her in daylight. But he wanted to see her.

"I know! " he shouted with glee, before breaking into a run.

He wanted to see her and he'll visit her, but he won't let her see him, would he?, yes, he won't, he'll hide.

A small drop of guilt grew inside him, but his desire to see her is greater.

He run and run until he reached the cliff ,just behind it will be dianne's cabin.

He took the sharp turn passing the cliff.

His smile faded on what he saw. The cabin.

It was in ruins,but he remebered it in perfect condition last night.He and Dianne even shared Dinner inside it by the fire that he made himself. It was nothing as he remembers it. Thin wooden pillars were either fallen down or burried in the sand, the Pier was broken, small planks scattered on the shore.

"What happened" Rusty asked lowly, dropping the flowers on the sand.

"Dianne? " he called out, but nothing. Only the soft whisper of the winds is present.

"Dianne! " he called out again, but no one seemed to hear him.

CHAPTER 18

"**W**illy?!,WILLY!" Rusty cried out, as he stormed inside the grocery.

"Willy!" he cried even louder.

"Lower your voice!" Willy shouted just as loud but more bone rattling, he appeared from the dark row of aisles.

"The cabin, what happened" Rusty pointed at the cabin's direction.

"Y-you know?" Willy asked lowly, his eyes, cold and blank laid on Rusty.

"It's not like that yesterday evening" Rusty clapped his forehead. "And Dianne! She's not there, where is she?" Rusty demanded an answer, grasping Willy's arms. Willy faced him frozen, as if afraid if he moved he'll break Rusty.

"Dianne is gone" Willy stared straight at Rusty.

"Gone where?, what have you done to her?!, if she left she will probably tell me" Rusty Shook Willy hard, but Willy didn't budged even a little.

"Have you seen the flowers?" Willy asked. Rusty stared at him bewildered.

"This is not the time to talk about that" Rusty said his eyes bulging out thier sockets.

"Sit first boy" Willy pulled him by the shoulder ,Rusty flicked his hand away. Pursing his lips. "SIT. BOY" Willy's growly voice thundered. Rusty melted on the command and allowed Willy to maneuver him into the counter.

Willy motioned a stool just afront the counter, Rusty sat at it while Willy takes his own seat at the stool inside the counter.

"Have you seen the flowers? " Willy asked again.

"THIS. IS. NOT. THE. TIME" Rusty breathed heavily.

"Answer me boy" Willy demanded, his eyes flashing faintly in the darkness.

"Yes, but, why would- ,yes"

It was Willy's turn to breath heavy, he rested his elbow on the counter and gazed at Rusty, "I planted the flowers in her honour"

What is he saying?, why would he honour Dianne.

"What do you mean"

A lone tear appeared on the corner of Willy's eye, sparkling like a gem of darkness. "Dianne is gone" he repeated.

"What do you mean? "

"The girl had perished"

Rusty stared at him sharply, this isn't the best joke he heard. "Stop fooling me! "

"The girl had perished!, an illness infected her, she grew weak. She stopped visiting the grocery. I thought it's my time to visit her, but when I did, I found her weak on the floor"

"No, that can't be!, you're pulling my leg right?, we played by the shore last night, she's perfectly alive" Rusty made an unconvincing smile.

"Before she pass, she asked me not tell anyone what happened to her, especially you. It didn't took long of course, the people noticed Dianne is gone"

"No! Lies! All lies! " Rusty screamed unable to take it all.

But pain speared through him, he took a run and Out the grocery. He can feel the tears growing at his lower lid. There were a lot of people, but he didn't care, he took a run not noticing them as they stared at him with judging eyes, a man running that fast must be being chased by the police.

He took a sharp turn into the dark wet fish market near the docks. It was vacant of people, he never took a second to notice the fishy smell on the air. He just ran. Rusty's heart raised beats, Sweat forming on his forehead, the muscles on his calves hardened. He breathed hard as he took the stone stairs of the docks. He'll reach the cabins eventually.

And with that, he did saw the cabins from afar, but instead took a turn tracing the wet lines on the shore.

Rusty stumbled on a large driftwood and fall on the ground. He crushed the sand on his palms as he tried to get up, sand sticking to his hair and the tip of his nose. He pushed his body up and started running again, gasping for air.

He reached the cabin almost out of breath. He fell on the sand stomach down, sand sticked to his clothes. His back rised and fell as he took in air ,which seemed not to fill his lungs, he tried breathing hard but just can't breath, Rusty's body begun to get numb, his fingers tightened, he felt his head getting lighter. Rusty blacked out, the only sound he heard was the slow waves and his own heavy breathing.

"Rusty" a demured whisper rung on his ear, a hand patting his back lightly.

Rusty woke up and stared at the figure kneeling in front of him, a girl with black hair and white dress, he need not to wait for his vision to clear up ,he knew.

"Dianne" he jolted up to embrace her, her hair tickled his face, her flowery scent reached his nose.

Orange lights hit them, the sea had became gold, the sun turned red. He must have passed out for hours.

Rusty released her and cupped her cheeks, there were rivers of tears on Dianne's face. Rusty wiped it with his thumb tenderly, but his own tears begun to fall themselves.

Dianne stood up and helped him get up. Her hair blown by the breeze, swaying and dancing in every direction. She reached out for his hand. Rusty gave it, squeezing her pale palms lightly.

"Is it true?" He asked lowly.

"I've waited for you Rusty " she smiled at him.

"Is it? " he repeated

Dianne stared at him but didn't answer. She pulled his hands as they slowly walked the beach. Sunlight kissed them both, warming their viens as blood circulates in them. A lump had started to grow in Rusty's throat ,he swallowed to get rid of it. This afternoon was the most beautiful Rusty had ever seen, the ivory skies above them sparkled and shined. They left their prints on the wet sand as they make way into a Cliff, behind the cabin.

The cliff was made of limestone, white in colour rough in texture. Under the Cliff lies a pile of Stones. Shells and washed up corals had been placed as well, the sea stones and corals had turned white. Washed by the weather and time.

"But this can't be" Rusty said staring at the piles of stone.

Dianne also stared at the pile of Stones, she sniffled and knodded slowly.

"All... All this time? " Rusty asked, tears now flowing out from his eyes.

"I wanted to keep my promise" she collapsed on his chest sobbing. "Thank you for fulfilling yours" Dianne stared at him, she placed her lips on his, warmth filling thier beings, she pulled her self away, and rested her hands on Rusty's face. Dianne slowly removed the ring off her neck and placed it on Rusty's palm. Rusty pulled him back into an embrace .He closed his eyes, tears dripping down his chin. He felt Dianne melt slowly in his embrace. He opened his eyes to see Dianne slowly being carried away by the breeze, as if she was a pile of dust, she slowly melted into thin air as the breeze carried her warm face ,disappearing into oblivion.

"I love you Rusty, I will always love you. Don't cry now, we have fulfilled our promises, be happy" the breeze in Dianne's voice whispered to Rusty.

"I... I love you Dianne" he said sobbing, clutching the gold ring in his palm, pushing it deep in his chest.

Rusty collapsed on the ground, lying in his back he stared at the darkening sky, stars had appeared, twinkling their little lights. He and Dainne had shared this sky once, and they will share it forever. He held the ring on his fingers, and pushed it near his heart.

He sighed, stopping the tears in his eyes, he laid on the sand unmoving, under the thousand beating hearts. Remembering their moments, the moments he had with the girl on the shore.

EPILOGUE

"No wonder you like this place, this place is great" said George, as he looks around the beach.

Rusty and his family had traveled from Rocco to Mortiana. Rusty was wearing the ring-necklace on his neck, it shines as the giddy sun strike them with rays of light.

"We'll be stopping here first" Rusty said as they got near the cluster of cabins. He stood in front of the biggest cabin and knocked.

"Wait a minute" a man said playfully from the inside . The door opened quickly, as Rowlin step outside. He had a large feline grin on his mouth.

"Hello Rowlin" Rusty greeted. Rowlin's eyes traveled from him and into the people behind him "oh, this is my family, Lucy, George and William"

"Great to meet the lovely people that raised this great man" Rowlin knodded courtly at them and placed a hand on Rusty's shoulder.

"Listen, Rusty, I'm very sorry" Rowlin started.

"For what? "

"I avoided you cause I was too embarrassed, I told you I'll look after Dianne, but I-i had an expedition on the neighboring city, and and when I... When I returned she passed on" Rowlin said lowly, his eyes shaking.

Rusty stared at him, he smiled gently. It's been months since he knew. "It's okay Rowlin, I'm not mad or anything"

Rowlin smirked at him. His eyes still sorry.

"So.. We are heading to the-" Rusty pointed the direction of Dianne's cabin with his thumb. "We'll get going then"

"Oh, matter of factly I was going there myself, I and a friend wanted to visit her" Rowlin said, "I just need something" he quickly entered his cabin.

Rusty waited outside and not a long moment after Rowlin came, he tied his red hair into a loose ponytail, he had his boots on.

"Shall we then? " Rusty asked everyone.

They knodded in unison. They started thier walk beside the shore. The sun above them was shining warmly, blue calm seas sent cool salty breeze, the bluer skies is full of thick cotton clouds.

When they reached the pile of stones. A man was already there, a fresh bouquet of roses in his hands.

"Oi! Willy! " Rowlin shouted, Willy turned around, an unusual smile on his face. Rusty never knew Willy could smile, his face was bathed in sunlight, he seemed younger and less intimidating. Less scarred as well.

"Took you long enough" Willy said voice still growly.

"I met them on the way" Rowlin answered.

Willy knodded at all of them, a warm smile present on his lips. They smiled back and gathered at the side of the stone piles.

"We were going to plant more bayhops today" Willy said staring at a whitened coral on the pile "we could use a bit of help"

"Sure " Rusty answered.

"I'll get the bayhops" William offered, Willy courtly knodded. "Race with me George" he shouted and bolted into a sprint.

"No fair! " George said and launched himself as well.

Rusty chuckled, staring at them and into the sea, the waves brings back memories, his feet melted as his mind replayed the sunsets they shared together.

"She's in a better place now dear, be happy for her" Lucy said, patting his arm, she joined him stare into the nothingness of the horizon.

"I am happy for her."